Flash Fiction Funny

82 Very Short Humorous Stories

Edited by Tom Hazuka

Blue Light Press ◆ 1st World Publishing

San Francisco ◆ Fairfield ◆ Delhi

FLASH FICTION FUNNY

1ST WORLD LIBRARY
PO Box 2211
Fairfield, Iowa 52556
www.1stworldpublishing.com

BLUE LIGHT PRESS
www.bluelightpress.com
Email: bluelightpress@aol.com

AUTHOR PHOTO
Christine Perkins-Hazuka

BOOK & COVER DESIGN
Melanie Gendron

FIRST EDITION

LCCN: 2013950665

ISBN 9781595408822

This book is dedicated to my students at Central Connecticut State University, with sincere appreciation for the listening and the laughing.

Contents

Bruce Holland Rogers

Egypt

The elder son went before his father and said unto him, "Let me go to the concert next Saturday, for the band is to be Good Charlotte."

And the Old Man said, "Who are you to go to any concert on Saturday when you have been grounded two weeks? And why is the lawn, which ought to have been mowed yesterday, still untouched by any blade?"

And in the morning at breakfast, the father could not drink of his coffee for it tasted of rust, and he complained bitterly to his wife.

And the son said, "Did I not ask you to let me go to the concert? Now the water is turned to rust."

But the father's heart was hard, and he said unto the mother, "Run the cold water a bit to clear the pipes before you make coffee."

And in the evening of the same day, when the father put his feet up to read the paper, there arose a great cry from the living room. "What in God's name?" said the father, and went to see his wife who stood pointing at a frog on the coffee table.

And the younger son was called to make an account of the frog, and he was made to take it back outside.

And the older son said, "Did I not ask you to let me go to the concert?"

And the next morning, there arose again a great cry, this time from the bathroom where the mother was combing the hair of the younger son. "Lice again?" said the father. "They need to fumigate those kids. I have had it about up to here with that school!"

And the older son said, "It is not the school that keeps me from going to the concert."

But the father's heart was hard, and he gave his son such a look.

And in the evening of the same day, the father said, "Who left the screen door standing open? The house is *full* of flies!"

And the son said, "Let me go to the concert, for all the guys will be there and I alone of all the guys will not."

And the father said, "You should have thought of that before you went and got yourself grounded."

And upon the morning of the next day, the car would not start, and the father tried to get a ride from a neighbor, but the neighbor's car also was afflicted.

And the father said, "I guess I will have to take the bus."

And the mother said, "Wait a second. What's that on your nose? Honey, you've got a pimple."

And the father said, "Oh, and at my age!"

And the sky darkened, and there was hail, very grievous, such as there was none like it upon the land since last summer.

And the hail smote the windshield of the car that would not start.

And the son said, "Let me go to the concert, else, if you refuse me, I will this afternoon bring locusts into the house."

But the father made no answer, and when he returned at the end of the day, on the kitchen counter he found empty milk jugs, cookie packages, yogurt cups, ice cream cartons, soda cans, and candy wrappers, for the son's friends had been over after school.

And that night, which was to be a night of watching television as a family, a thick darkness befell the room and they saw not one another nor the TV, and the mother said, "Looks like the whole neighborhood is out."

And the son said, "Let me go to the concert, for I am bored out of my skull."

But the father said, "Pester me no more on this and take heed to thyself; ask not again, for in that hour you ask me again, from that hour will you be grounded until your eighteenth birthday."

And upon the morning of the Saturday, the son had such a headache, like unto death, and he moaned most grievously for his parents who had not granted him his dying wish and the guilt they must henceforth bear.

But the father's heart was harder than the heart of Pharaoh.

And it came to pass that the son listened to the songs of Good Charlotte on his iPod alone in his room, and he did not die.

Julianna Baggott

The Prude Responds to Rock and Roll

I have legs but don't know how to use them. I'm out of sugar but if I had some, I would not lend you any nor would I feel comfortable pouring some on you.

I'm not a beauty and that's not all right. It's upsetting. When I think about you I don't touch myself or if I do it's only to readjust the Kleenex up my sleeve.

My body isn't a wonderland. It's more like a wicker furniture showroom.

I don't own a fruit cage, to my knowledge. (What's a fruit cage?)

When you claim you'll take me to a place I've never been before, which, can I mention, you say a lot, I do need you to be specific before I consent.

And yet part of me inexplicably irreversibly wants you to want me—because regardless it's been too long. In fact, it's been a very long time—a long, long time. It's been long and lonely—a lonely lonely lonely (oh, so lonely) time.

Joey Comeau

Cover Letter

Dear Sirs or Madams!

I am enclosing my résumé in the hopes that you will consider me for a position with Nova Magnetics. My résumé details my experience with magnet technical sales, but I would like to take some time to explain my other qualifications as well. I have a very special relationship with magnetic sales, and with magnets in particular. When I was a child I accidentally consumed a small fridge magnet in the shape of a kitten. Due to the magnet's odd shape, it has not passed through my system. It is lodged in my intestines somewhere or other, and I hope to god that it stays there. Why? Because it gives me special powers.

These powers aren't related to magnets. I can't make metal hover, or anything you might find in a comic book. No. But I have always known I was different. I have abilities that set me apart from others. I have powers. Do you know anyone who can see perfectly in the dark? I'll bet you do. What's special about that? Cats can do it. Owls. Heck, my little brother has abnormally high night vision. But do you know anyone who goes completely blind if the sun even goes behind a cloud? I do. Me.

But that's the least of my powers. I have others. For example, I have a form of ESP that allows me to consistently pick losing lottery numbers, and generally make poor life choices. I used to rub these powers in other people's faces. I had a shirt made up that says, "I consistently make poor life choices." It was not popular, but that is how great my powers are. Did I mention my other powers? I can come up with T-shirt slogans on the spot.

"Kiss me, I have no night vision."

"I can't even think correctly!"

"This womb drops babies!"

But I realize that while these powers give my life the sheen of wonder, and they are born of the magnet lodged in my intestines, they might not convince you that I can be a good technical sales guy. Well, I assure you that I can! If you would like to speak with me about this position, I would ask that we meet in person. I do not own a telephone, because I do not trust them. You can't see the other person! It could be anyone. Did you see Terminator 2, where the robot imitates the mother's voice and HE KILLED HER?

No way, man. If you want to hire me we're going to have to meet up somewhere. I think McDonald's is a good place. There's lots of people, and I feel safe there. Meet me there at three o'clock Thursday morning if you're interested. I feel my qualifications would make me a valuable addition to your team! I look forward to meeting you at McDonald's in order to learn more while not being murdered by a robot from the future.

Yours,
Joey Comeau

Taylor Mali

The the Impotence of Proofreading

Has this ever happened to you? You work very horde on a paper for English clash and then get a very glow raid (like a D or even a D=) and all because you are the word's liverwurst spoiler. Proofreading your peppers is a matter of the the utmost impotence.

This is a problem that affects manly, manly students. I myself was such a bed spiller once upon a term that my English torturer in my sophomoric year, Mrs. Myth, said I would never get into a good colleague. And that's all I wanted, just to get into a good colleague. Not just anal community colleague, because I wouldn't be happy at anal community colleague. I needed a place that would offer me intellectual simulation, I really need to be challenged, challenged menstrually. I know this makes me sound like a stereo, but I really wanted to go to an ivory legal colleague. So I needed to improvement poor gone would be my dream of going to Harvard, Jail, or Prison (in Prison, New Jersey).

So I got myself a spell checker and figured I was on Sleazy Street.

But there are several missed aches that a spell chukker can't can't catch catch. For instant, if you accidentally leave a word your spell exchequer won't put it in you. And God for billing purposes only you should have serial problems with Tori Spelling your spell Chekhov might replace a word with one you had absolutely no detention of using. Because what do you want it to douch? It only does what you tell it to douche. You're the one with your hand on the mouth going clit, clit, clit. It just goes to show you how embargo one careless clit of the mouth can be.

Which reminds me of this one time during my Junior Mint. The teacher read my entire paper on A Sale of Two Titties out loud to all of my assmates. I'm not joking, I'm totally cereal. It was the most humidifying experience of my life, being laughed at pubically.

So do yourself a flavor and follow these two Pisces of advice. One: There is no prostitute for careful editing. And three: When it comes to proofreading, the red penis your friend.

PAMELA PAINTER

ARTIST AS GUEST IN THE HAMPTONS

First of all, his wife informed him, we can't possibly have the Horstels to dinner with the Jimm Smythhs because the long dining room wall—the only space large enough for the 6' by 15' paintings they each gave us—is occupied, so to speak. Hanging there is that sixty pound oil and gouache titled "Whale and Water" that Xu Xi announced was her "house-gift" in the thank you note she sent express mail a month after her three week stay. Remember, since she used real glass "Whale and Water" was too heavy when we tried to lug it down to the basement.

He remembered all too well. Besides, he was still feeling the after-effects of last fall's hernia from carrying the Lindstrom bronze porpoise down from the potting shed to the patio when Sven Lindstrom mentioned he was coming to visit them in the Hamptons to reinvigorate his artistic vision. And no doubt acquire another muse, his wife said. So in addition to having the Horstels and Smythhs separately to dinner we'll have to wait till our roaming son Charlie is home from his RISD internship to unseat the Xu Xi and haul either the Horstel or Smythh up from the basement, depending on the guest list, to the "place of honor" in the dining room. There the artist was always circumspectly seated across from his or her work, which occasionally had a stultifying effect on conversation, but could also lead to some interesting anecdotes, like the story Tioni used to tell before he died about his painted wooden leg's adventures in Italy. Lord knows where in the garage Tioni's "Afternoon of the Fun" is buried.

Meanwhile, his wife said, about tomorrow's dinner party: the small, lush Klayton watercolor—let's see, that was his house gift four years ago—should probably be moved from the guest bathroom to the entranceway, though it does match the new marble tiles perfectly, and goodness, we can't forget to bring his wife's multi-colored, jelly-bean platter down from the attic, though we still aren't sure Janine didn't mean it as a joke. And we must call the art restorer to see if he's replaced the matting on the Binner, since they're good friends of the Horstels, and also ask if he was able to disinfect the canvas so there is no hint of Nero's recurring bladder problem. It proved so ruinous to the Mendoza triptych that we can only dine out with them, and of course pick up the check year after year after year.

And by the way, his wife said, the Hampton Art Museum called to remind us that we still haven't retrieved the Missy Massey painting that we'd donated to their auction last year. We told her we were donating it, so heaven forbid she asks what it went for. The director suggested that requiring the opening bid begin at $100 might have been a bit high. Surely, her husband said wistfully, someone might be at this year's art auction who really loves Peoria, as in "I 'Heart' Peoria," since the Finleys have stopped speaking to us ever since Finn found his "I 'Heart' Frogs" behind the ficus in the library. Or was it in the closet?

What is this anyway, his wife said, why can't these artists arrive with two exquisite ripe cheeses? Or, he said, a vintage Bordeaux or a good bottle of champagne—house gifts, they agreed, that would disappear at evening's end into the Hamptons' own starry night.

Ron Carlson

Syllabus

There will be four papers in this course, three informal response papers to the text, and one research paper that will be on one of the selected topics. The research paper will include ten footnotes applied in the manner of the Sheboygan Style Guide available in the Department Office on the eleventh floor of Lincoln Hall. Any students who object to using footnotes should see me for accommodation. Any students with ongoing addictions to controlled and uncontrolled substances should plan ingestion schedules so as to avoid any awkwardness Tuesdays and Thursdays 1:30 to 4:00 p.m. in our classroom, the Agribusiness Cultural Auditorium. Any students with concealed weapon permits should plan on leaving those weapons at home. Students may carry concealed weapon permits onto the campus. Neo Nazi students need not see me. Members of the Student Society for Cranial Tattoos need not see me. Students on Rogaine, Viagra, or any of the local versions of crystal methamphetamine should see me for accommodation. Students who are currently being stalked should fill out the blue half-page stalking form in the department office; without that form, we can make no accommodation. Students who are actively stalking someone, male or female, should keep a notebook or a journal with page numbers so that this material could be used in the research paper footnotes (see above). Students who are active members of Spirits of the Pentagram or the locally franchised Satan Says discussion groups should see me so that we can make accommodations. Students whose family circumstances include long-term generational feuds and continuing sporadic gunfire from behind trees in the hills of their hometowns should see me for accommodation. Students who are ranking officers in community militias should see me for accommodation. Active members of the press should expect a B in this course. Tops. Any student with full brains should see me for accommodation. Clones, robots and students who are from other planets should see me for accommodation.

Students who have suffered from Spontaneous Human Combustion should sit near the exits and select the purple fireproof handout packets. Any students who are related to the university president, the president's cousin who teaches in our department, or any members of the department's personnel committee should see me for accommodation.

In this classroom open flames, flagrant sexual activity, and gambling with dice or cards are discouraged. A second warning on any of these could get a student a yellow caution in the suggestion folder.

Attendance is optional, but call in from time to time. All phone calls will be monitored. Let's have a good semester.

On those footnotes: if ten is too many, nine would work. Eight minimum.

Jon Davis

Music Men

Chris Isaak arrives early in yellow swim trunks, a bright towel hanging like a horseshoe around his neck. He's been on the beach with two supermodels-in-training. They're with him now as he looks for a piano. Suddenly, a diaphanous song materializes above him. He whispers into its ear. It follows him into the studio, clacking on its oversized heels.

Van Morrison arrives late, coughing into his fist. He spent the night on Cypress Avenue. A pale woman in a large black hat, her thin arms festooned with bracelets, floats behind him. He needs a guitar right now. A song is pouring out of his chest. He catches it in the sound hole of the guitar.

Chris Isaak has his people call for an arugula salad, with cranberries and walnuts and thinly sliced ahi, a bottle of champagne. He passes out chopsticks to the supermodels-in-training. They circle the salad as if it were an altar to loveliness and success. Chris Isaak lights a candle. They all laugh and eat. With chopsticks, Chris Isaak plucks an arugula leaf stuck to one woman's pouty lower lip.

Van Morrison becomes famished. He discovers a lamb in the meadow behind the studio. He slaughters it with a tenor saxophone. A single blow to the head. He butchers it, lays a fire using old Decca labels and peat, then roasts the lamb on a rock he sets in the middle of the fire. Lustily does he eat the lamb, slipping chunks also into the red mouth of his woman.

Chris Isaak has a pallet made on the floor. He puts a sleep mask on. The supermodels-in-training curl beside him. They lay their heads carefully on his chest, facing each other. Chris Isaak places his hands lightly on their heads, slipping his fingers into their hairstyles. They sleep.

Van Morrison must slumber. He flops on the floor. Pulls his woman down with him. Together, they kick at things—dishes, books, guitars, horn charts, discarded lyrics—until they've cleared enough space. Van Morrison pulls the small woman to his chest. Holds her tight until dawn.

Chris Isaak is feeling it and the musicians arrive. They uncase their instruments. Tune. Chris Isaak runs over the lyric. It's about two supermodels-in-training. Palm trees. Laughing and drinking champagne. During the bridge they all roll in the wet sand. But one of the women has left Chris Isaak. The other won't tolerate his advances. He aches for one, longs for the other, talks to neither. O, sweet conundrum. His voice quavers with it. He's never been happier.

Van Morrison wants to record. He calls up a saxophonist, a drummer, and a bass player. The saxophonist's instrument has been run over by a truck. The drummer was recently blinded in a chemical spill. The bass player is homeless. Van counts it off, lays out the chords. "Hut" he shouts and the drummer whacks the tom. He's whispering where they thought he would sing, crooning where they thought he would growl, growling where they thought he'd call for a solo. The woman in the black hat is lost to swaying. She takes a long solo with her hips and shoulders. Outside the surviving lambs are bleating. Rain slaps the roof like a tambourine.

Sarah Russell

Mother's Last Wishes

Dear Children,

These are my final requests.

Jeff, since the accident of your impending birth led to my marrying your father, I am putting you in charge of parceling out what is left of the estate. Try to be more fair to your siblings than your father was to me.

Susan, you have always been good at arranging things, like that abortion you never told me about, so you are in charge of my cremation. I have no intention of lying next to that man in a burial plot like I had to for thirty-eight years—or alone in an urn for that matter. Let my ashes find a bit of freedom in the wind. You should understand as you have chosen freedom over giving me grandchildren.

Jack—Jackson—you have always been my favorite, you know. But although I told you that you were named for a great-uncle, that is not the case. In Morristown, you will find a Jackson Tulley listed in the phone book. He has waited thirty-two years to meet you.

Regarding my funeral, go to no more trouble than you did when you sent me to hospice rather than taking me into one of your homes. No maudlin songs or scripture. Just say I was a woman to whom life dealt a pair of deuces in a high stakes game, and that I bluffed as best I could.

Advice? Don't settle. It will devour you.

As ever,
Mother

Colin McEnroe

Primitive Man Tames the Wolf

Report of Advisory Committee on Wolf Domestication: A Blueprint for Responsible Change

Chairman: Man Who Looks Like Tree

Vice-Chair: Woman Who Lives on Ledge

Committee members: Woman Who Smells Bad, Man Who Smells Even Worse, Man Who Loves Show Tunes, Woman Who Eats Bugs, Hairy Person With Small Feet

ABSTRACT: For years, people in tribe ask: Why wolf hate us? Why wolf steal our food? Can't we and wolf get along? Some people say: forget about it. You never tame wolf. Someday, people go in tent and sit in big circle and watch lion do tricks, watch tiger do tricks, watch bear do tricks. Never wolf. Still wolf hang around. We decide try be friends with wolf. Maybe work and live with wolf.

Project I. HERE, WOLF!

Concept: Invite wolf join campfire group. Methodology: Everybody stand at edge of darkness waving wild pig meat and say: Here, wolf. Nice pig meat! Here, wolf!

Result: Wolf run in from darkness, take baby, run away. Conclusion: Concept need retooling.

Project II. COOPERATIVE HUNTING

Concept: Rabbits good to eat but run so fast. Faster than people. Faster than wolf.

What if we help wolf and wolf help us? Methodology: Start on one side of rabbit-rich target area. Chase rabbits toward wolves. Results: At first go well. Rabbits run toward wolves and wolves catch. Experiment team say: OK, now share. Wolves growl and bite people who come near. Eat almost all rabbits. (See scatter diagram attached.) People get two old rabbits who die of fear. Slow cook in broth with wild beans, grains, grasses. Can stretch to feed 73. Nearly unanimous vote to make recipe part of oral tradition. Dissenting vote: Woman with Shiny Stones the vegan.

Project III. FETCH

Concept: Maybe wolf like play game. Methodology: Throw stick. Hypothesis: Wolf bring stick back. Repeat. Hours of fun. Results: Flat-Headed Far-Throwing Man throw stick. Wolf locate stick, sniff to see if food. Wolf not pleased. Conclusion: Services for Flat-Headed Far-Throwing Man handled quite tastefully, in panel's opinion. Wild lily arrangements very attractive and Griot's sermon: "He Had Some Good Times; Now Let's Divide Up His Meager Possessions" really hit sharp fastening object on head.

Project IIII. SHEEPADOODLE

Concept: Maybe wolf just too mean. What if combine with quiet, easy animal? Like sheep! Sheep no trouble at all. What could go wrong? Methodology: Catch wolf. Put in cave with sheep. Dim campfire. Assemble tribe outside cave for ancient magical chant: Can't get enough of your love, babe. Oh, no. Result: create new animal called IDS (Incredibly Dangerous Sheep). IDS worse than wolf in some ways. Stand there looking innocent then attack and bite and stomp. Upside: Large flock of IDS rampage against nearby Tribe Who Dress In Crow Feathers, who get on nerves of this tribe. Or did. Comment from elders: You can say the log segment with the hollowed-out area from which water can be drunk is half-empty or you can say the blah-blah woof-woof is half-full.

HIATUS: Project team disassemble for Festival of When Moon Look a Certain Way And We Thank Gods in Sky for Not Destroying Us. Fermented berry beverages. Dancing to 30 goatskin drums. Project team members all agree: carrying a lot of tension around. Really good to blow off steam.

Project IIII. FIND STUPID NICE WOLF

Concept: Maybe not all wolves created equal. Methodology: Find wolf who is kind of loser. Left out of many wolf activities. Wolf with no life. Get loser wolf to enjoy people. Results: Very good plan. Found wolf no other wolfs like. Brought wolf to campfire. Named him Al the Wolf. Then make up new word. Al the Dog. That way maybe Al forget he is wolf.

Comments: Al the Dog very nice but not big help. Always hungry. Want people scratch head. Scared of rabbits. Stand far away and make noise at them. When man come to bring tree-paper messages from other tribes, Al bite him. Must give message man 100 beans to calm down. Then Al get sick. Throw up all day. Women very worried. Poor Al the Dog! Take to shaman who cure Al with rattles and dust. Make us give 300 beans. Say after hours. Emergency rate. Leave Al near cave while go gather more beans. Come back and find Al tear up things we sleep on. Women say he just nervous.

Project IIIII. GET AL ADOPTED

Concept: Free to good tribe. Come get. Don't send tree-paper message man. He not deliver here now.

Peter Cherches

Double Date

It's a Shakespearean double date—Hamlet and Ophelia and Macbeth and Lady Macbeth go to a restaurant, a steak house. It turns into a comedy of errors. As soon as they arrive, Lady Macbeth heads to the ladies' room to wash her hands, and she stays in there for twenty minutes. And Ophelia's such a weirdo—in the middle of a conversation she starts singing snatches of old songs. Then, every time the waiter comes to take their order, Hamlet says he needs a few more minutes to decide. When they're finally ready to order, it turns out that Hamlet and Ophelia don't even want steak—Ophelia orders the California Platter and Hamlet says, "I'll just have a Danish." The Macbeths are big meat eaters, though, and they both ask for the 16-ounce New York cut. Macbeth orders his medium rare but Lady Macbeth wants hers well done—the sight of blood nauseates her. While they're waiting for the food to come the Macbeths try to make small talk, but it's a losing proposition—Hamlet is sullen and morose and Ophelia's in her own world. When the food finally arrives there's another problem—both steaks are well done.

"Call the waiter," Lady Macbeth says. "Tell him to take it back."

"That's all right, dear," Macbeth says. "I'll eat this one."

"You ordered medium rare!"

"Yes, but I don't want to make a scene."

"Don't be such a wimp," Lady Macbeth says. "Send it back!"

"All right, dear," Macbeth says, and motions for the waiter.

When the waiter gets to their table, he insists that both Macbeths ordered their steaks well done.

"Are you going to take that from this prick?" Lady Macbeth screeches.

"No, dear," Macbeth replies, and kills the waiter.

Hamlet, who has just taken the first bite of his Danish, spits it out all over the table. "Yecch," he says. "Something's rotten."

On top of everything else, the Macbeths drink so much coffee that they might as well kiss the idea of sleep good night.

Mandy Manning

Just Outside the Closet

Cinderella stood just outside the closet.

"Again with the damn shoes?" she said. "I can see you, you know."

Prince Charming sat on the floor with Cinderella's glass slipper in his hand. He licked the toe of the shoe. When she burst in, he almost dropped it.

She stood at the door with her hands on her hips. "What is wrong with you?"

Prince Charming's socks lay on the floor next to him. The hair on his legs was mashed haphazardly against his pale skin and he had a red elastic imprint on his upper calf. Cinderella's black pumps adorned his feet and he wasn't wearing any pants.

Cinderella snatched the slipper out of his hand. "You're going to break it!"

He tried to grab it back, managing only to touch it with one fingertip. His breath shortened and he swallowed hard. "I was just washing it. It had a little smudge on the toe."

Cinderella bent over and pulled the pumps from his feet. "You stretch them out when you do this." She placed them on the shelf.

"They slip off my heels when I walk."

"Put them on and show me." Prince Charming licked his lips.

Cinderella wrinkled her nose. "Gross! Knock it off!" She wiped the spittle from the glass slipper and placed it back onto the pillow next to its twin in the lockbox. "Where did you get the key?"

"Key?" Prince Charming struggled with his stockings. He'd put on a few pounds since the wedding and the socks were a little tight. His pants were also a bit snug, but he could still get them zipped if he sucked in.

Cinderella, on the other hand, had grown even more beautiful. She'd taken to jogging in the mornings to keep her waist trim, and the diamond tiara nestled in her hair brought out the amber flecks in her eyes. She held out her hand. "Give it to me."

"What?" He looped his belt around his waist, avoiding her eyes. She tapped her foot. "The key."

"What key?"

"Don't play stupid! The key to the lockbox."

Still not looking at her, he put his own shoes on, lacing them slowly. "I didn't use a key."

Cinderella whirled around and studied the lock. "You broke it."

Prince Charming stood up, put his hands on his hips, and nodded. "Yep!" He brushed past her. "You don't have a right to keep them locked up."

"Yes, I do!"

"No, you don't! They're as much mine as they are yours."

Cinderella followed him out of the closet. "How do you figure that?"

"They brought us together." He sat down on the edge of the bed, positioning himself so that he could see past Cinderella into the closet. Her shoes were lined up in their little cubbies. Perfect. He smiled.

"Wait a minute." Cinderella looked at the floor and shook her head. "What are you saying?"

"You did leave one behind. Don't play like you didn't know what that would do."

"I guess, I mean, you used the shoe to find me." She moved closer to him, blocking his view. He craned his neck to see around her again.

"No, I brought the slipper around to find the other shoe."

Cinderella looked again at the floor. "You mean you're not even interested in me at all?" Her face burned red. "Then why did you even marry me?"

"Don't be like that, Cindy. I had to marry you." He stood up and put his hands on her shoulders. "No one wears the slippers like you." He looked into her eyes and shook his head. "Believe me, I've tried."

"So, you just wanted the shoes?"

"No." He turned her toward the closet. "I want your feet in the shoes." He gave her a little push. "Go and put them on."

Cinderella's shoulders drooped. She lowered her head and walked into the closet. The lockbox was still ajar. She reached in and took out the slippers. For a moment she held the shoes above her head as if she might smash them.

"You do like being a princess, don't you?" Prince Charming sat on the bed watching her.

Cinderella slowly lowered the shoes and slipped them onto her feet.

Removing his own shoes, Prince Charming called to her, "Bring the black pumps, too."

Ronald G. Crowe

Brothers and Sisters

"Brothers and sisters, I stand before you this morning with a heavy heart and a troubled mind, for this Lord's servant has been accused of *awful things*. But do I quake with fear? Do I stand here shamed? No, brethren, I am here to tell you those charges are false, mean-hearted, slanderous, and unworthy of true Christian believers. Oh, judge not, lest ye also be judged!

"I forgive the deacons. I even forgive that *Anchorage Daily News* reporter who wrote such scurrilous things about me. Yea, I love and forgive those who would bring me down! You may ask, as does my own dear wife of 30 years, who sits weeping among you: How is it, Reverend Stiffles, that the Reverend Jerry Falvo took a picture of you in *flagrante delicto* with a young woman in the back room of the Loving Hands Massage Parlor? And that same picture appeared on the front page of the *Anchorage Daily News* just yesterday?

"Oh, brothers and sisters! I'm glad these misunderstandings have surfaced! Now I can explain them and put your minds to rest. Here is what really happened:

"When driving, I like to practice my sermons. But a man shouting loudly to himself in the car, waving his arms, etc., tends to attract curious looks from other drivers. It has at times caused me embarrassment. Well, I took this problem to the Lord, and he told me all I needed was a life-size dummy to put in the passenger's seat beside me. Then, when I practiced preaching, people would think I was talking to a companion.

"Well, I searched all over for such a dummy, but could only find one at this little shop over in Spenard where they sell uh—adult health aids. This dummy could be inflated by a valve in its—yes there was a valve in this lady look-alike dummy. I inflated her at a gas station and sat her up in the car seat. I was driving home when, "pssst!" Alas, my inflatable lady had sprung a leak. Well, I stopped at what looked like a health spa to me, where the gracious lady in charge found me a Band-Aid and let me use the back room where I could lay my dummy on the bed and fix her—well, patch her leak.

"That is precisely what I was doing when that Reverend Jerry Falvo snuck around like a thief in the night and rudely took my picture through the back window.

"I realize the photograph made my dummy look like a real young woman in a state of undress. But you must realize how realistic these inflatable dummies look today. I understand perfectly well how the mistake was made. To err is human, brethren.

"Now I know from your mutterings that there are still some doubting Thomases out there asking, why don't I produce that punctured, inflatable doll to support my story? Brethren, I would gladly do so, but you see, by the time the leak was fixed, the dummy had lost most of her air. So I took her back to the gas station to inflate again. Well, as I was putting air into her, I saw this woman crossing the street and thought she was a member of our congregation. While my attention was diverted, I overinflated the doll, blew its patch. And just like a toy balloon, the escaping air propelled the doll straight up—I mean, amazingly high! At that moment a floatplane had taken off from Lake Spenard, and, unbelievably, it caught the dummy on one of its floats. So the last I saw of it, it was flapping like a rag doll in the wind as the bush plane climbed and headed out over Cook Inlet.

"So there it is, brothers and sisters. And I only ask that you again give me a small benefit of the doubt as you did so graciously last year when those unholy rumors were circulating about me and our former organist Miss Ilene Peebles.

"Brethren, you will find only innocence here. See no evil—hear no evil—think no evil. And may we again be united in brotherly love. And in the name of God and truth, may this clear the air once and for all. Now, let us pray."

Sholeh Wolpé

My Brother at the Canadian Border

For Omid

On their way to Canada in a red Mazda, my brother and his friend, PhDs with little sense, stopped at the border and the guard leaned forward, asked: Where you boys heading?

My brother, *Welcome to Canada* poster in his eyes, replied: *Mexico.* The guard blinked, stepped back then forward, said: *Sir, this is the Canadian border.* My brother turned to his friend, grabbed the map from his hands, slammed it on his shaved head. *You stupid idiot*, he yelled, *you've been holding the map upside down.*

In the interrogation room full of metal desks and chairs with wheels that squeaked and fluorescent light humming, bombarded with questions, and finally: *Race?*

Stymied, my brother confessed: *I really don't know, my parents never said.* The woman behind the desk widened her blue eyes to take in my brother's olive skin, hazel eyes, the blonde fur that covered his arms and legs. Disappearing behind a plastic partition, she returned with a dusty book, thick as *War and Peace.*

This will tell us your race. Where was your father born? she asked, putting on her horn-rimmed glasses.

Persia, he said.

Do you mean I-ran?

I ran, you ran, we all ran. He smiled.

Where's your mother from? Voice cold as a gun.

Russia, he replied.

She put one finger on a word above a chart in the book, the other on a word at the bottom of the page, brought them together looking like a mad mathematician bent on solving the crimes of zero times zero divided by one. Her fingers stopped on a word. Declared: *You are white.*

My brother stumbled back, a hand on his chest, eyes wide, mouth in an O as in *O my God! All these years and I did not know.* Then to the room, to the woman and the guards: *I am white. I can go anywhere. Do anything. I can go to Canada and pretend it's Mexico. At last, I am white and you have no reason to keep me here.*

DAVID SWANN

THE ABBA MOOR-WALKING SOCIETY

At the age of 12, I formed a moor-walking society with the pop group ABBA.

Our hikes were fueled by Benny and Bjorn, who prepared sandwiches sealed in foil triangles, packed with fudgy Norwegian cheese.

Sometimes I had to pinch myself that I was hiking with ABBA—but mostly I was too busy probing the mist for trig-points, or hopping over bogs, or seeking out trails.

Until, one day, Benny confessed he was finding the drizzle a *"leetle"* difficult.

Later, in Todmorden's best tearoom, we waved him farewell. For a time, the tearoom was heavy with absence. But then Anni-Frid ordered more scones.

"Come, child," she said. "Produce your map, and decide our next route."

"W. . . without Benny?"

Abba's three remaining members laughed. "Did you think we would leave you?"

"We sang the ballad *Fernando*," Agnetha sighed. "We know the agony of loss. If Benny goes solo, we must respect his wishes."

And so we tramped on over the moors, resigned to Benny's loss. But the rain pelted our faces, and Bjorn collapsed with a groan.

"Bjorn," said Anna-Frid, "what ails you?"

Bjorn began to weep. "I have a confession to make. For too long, I let you believe I prepared our picnics . . ."

"The fudgy Norwegian cheeses?" Agnetha gasped.

"Yes, the triangular sandwiches. They were made not by me, but by Benny."

I pushed to the front. "So Benny did *all* the packed lunches?"

Bjorn nodded, fisting away tears. "Although I wrapped them . . ."

But it was too late. We turned away. Without consulting the girls, I knew we agreed.

Looking back, I saw Bjorn shivering under a pylon.

"Was it just me," I asked the girls, "or did it seem weird to be with Bjorn and not Benny?"

"To be honest," said Anna-Frid, "I could never tell them apart."

We squinted into the rain, searching out a trail.

Soon afterwards, Anna-Frid fell into a bog.

I put my hands around Agnetha's waist. Together, we strained to pull Anna-Frid free. But the bog closed over her lovely brunette hair, and she slipped beneath the mire.

"She died here in the high places," said Agnetha, tears mixing with rain on her beautiful face. "It was a Scandinavian death."

Agnetha had always been the quietest moor-walker, and this was the most I had heard her say.

"Agnetha," I said, her name like a spell, "I must confess. When Bjorn left, I felt . . . felt . . ."

"Felt happy? Yes. Yes, we all did," she whispered. "For what was Bjorn without Benny? Or Benny without Bjorn? Or whichever?"

"And when Anna-Frid . . ."

Agnetha finished my speech. "When she sank, you saw a chance to be alone with me?"

I nodded, ashamed.

"We sang *Knowing Me, Knowing You*," said Agnetha. "We know the agonies of love."

"Poor Anna-Frid," I said, watching bubbles popping on the morass.

"Yes," said Agnetha. "Poor Anna-Frid. Who was your second favourite member. But who looked like your mother's best friend. The one with the comforting smile."

"Yes," I whispered.

"Come," said Agnetha—and her smile offered more than comfort—"let us continue our expedition."

"Just the two of us?"

She straightened her blonde hair, her face in profile, as I had seen it in the videos.

So it was that Agnetha and I hiked on, out of the valley beyond Bacup, through the cleft of Waterfoot, as far as the ridge above Helmshore . . . until, on high ground above Accrington, where wind cut flashes in the high grass, I mustered my courage and stood on tiptoes to plant a clumsy kiss upon her cheek.

"I'm sorry," I gasped, reluctantly releasing my hand from her back pocket.

Agnetha smiled gravely, but she understood. It was her vocal on *When I Kissed the Teacher*, after all.

I knew we had walked our final path, knew that we were fated to end like the lovers in their song, blue since the day they parted.

"Breaking up is never easy," Agnetha sighed. "But this is no place for a girl in white satin bell bottoms."

"The mud," I conceded glumly.

Above us, a helicopter appeared, shining down a bright spotlight. Agnetha stood yearning in that cone of light, her satin trousers flapping.

"Never forget our time together," she said.

"Never," I promised, and turned to face my town.

I looked back only once, to see Agnetha climbing that ladder of light. Soon she would be soaring above the drizzle, her beautiful eyes gone forever.

Ahead, amplifiers set on 11 were throbbing in garages, a brand new loneliness to roam and endure. Guitars screamed and distant drums pounded over the cinder tracks as I trudged home. It was Friday night. The lights were low, and I was looking out for a place to go.

Chuck Rosenthal

Intimations of Immortality

When I'm in my office at school I shut the door and talk to myself really loud so students will think I'm busy with someone else and not interrupt. I have a grad assistant assigned to empty my mailbox into the recycling bin. Email? Would you think I used my university address? But one day, expecting a call from my bookie, I picked up the phone.

"Professor Shark?" said a small voice. "My name is Rhonda Riordan and you are my advisor because you do the R's?"

"How did you get this number?"

"It says on my red advisee sheet—do you have my red sheet?"

"Why would I have your red sheet if you have your red sheet?"

"Because my name is Rhonda Riordan and you are my advisor because you do the R's?"

"What do you need to know?"

"It says here on my red sheet that I have to take both one course in English literature before 1800 and one after? Does that mean I have to take one course in English literature before 1800 and one after?"

"Would you accept yes as an answer?" I said.

"Both? Not one or the other?"

"What do you think both means?"

"One or the other?"

"It means both," I said.

"I mean," said Rhonda, "maybe they're saying both, but they mean one or the other."

"Who are they?" I said. "Who do you think they are?"

"I don't know," said Rhonda. "That's a good question. That could be something important to think about."

"What do *you* mean when you say both?" I asked.

"That's a good question, too. Maybe I would mean one or the other. It would certainly be better for me if it meant one or the other."

"Well, Rhonda Riordan, as your advisor I advise you to think that it means that you have to take one of each."

"Oh, I was afraid of that. Maybe I shouldn't have called. Do you know when 1800 is?"

"When?" I said.

"I mean, how do I know what's before and what's after?" said Rhonda in her small voice.

I tried to remain calm. After all, it was only my life I was wasting here and one needed to, if not enjoy it, at least concentrate on it, with detachment. "Anything lower than 1799 is before," I said. "1800 and up is after."

"So like the twentieth century is after?"

"That's right."

"The nineteenth?"

"After," I said.

"And the eighteenth is after then, right?"

"The eighteenth century is the 1700's," I said. "It's before."

"The eighteenth century is the 1700's! Oh my god! How can that be? Is that why everything is divided at 1800? Why do you people do that?"

"Us people?"

"Then there's this thing with fiction and nonfiction. How can something be non and true. Shouldn't fiction be about true stuff and nonfiction be made up?"

"Often it is," I said. "Maybe you should be a philosophy major."

"Do you think?" Rhonda asked.

"Yes," I said, "then you could get a philosophy advisor."

"But you are my advisor, Professor Shark. How can seventeen be called eighteen?"

"One to ninety-nine is the first century," I said.

"No!"

"Yes."

"Well that's the problem then," said Rhonda Riordan.

"Indeed," I said. I couldn't ever remember having said indeed before.

"Maybe you can fix it?"

"You'd still have to take something before or something after something."

"Has it always been this way?"

"Sadly, Rhonda Riordan, I think it has always been this way. It's a hard flower we all have to swallow."

"My heart!" said Rhonda Riordan.

Outside my door I heard the rising murmur of infinite student need, a line of advisees circling like a snake swallowing its tail. I put the receiver in its cradle with utter silence, so as not to prompt a cell phone of intent, or dialogue of business, love, or strife.

But the voices outside my door rose in unison. "Help us! Help us, Professor Shark! What is before? What is after? What is both?"

Francine Witte

Just Before I Shoot

I ask Thompson if he has a last request. Not that I'll honor it, but I'm curious.

He does a wormy, squirmy thing inside his thousand-dollar suit. "I'd like to call my wife," he says. I have to laugh, but only inside. I don't want to seem too flip.

I take the cell phone out of my Michael Kors handbag. The one I got on eBay. Very nice. The other office women always ooh and aah and want to stroke the nubby suede.

"What's the number?" I say. "I'll dial." I'm not afraid he'll call the cops, but who knows?

"I-I don't know," he says. He smells like he just crapped his pants.

"How do you not know your own wife's number?" This pisses me off in a gum-losing-its-flavor kind of a way.

"Speed dial," he says. "Number 4."

He is really beginning to stink up the place, so I take a pine tree air freshener out of my lovely purse and hang it from his right ear.

"Can't I use my own phone?" he asks. "It's in my pocket."

The thought of going anywhere near his pants disgusts me. "Never mind," I say. "I'll explain it to her at the funeral."

"I'm allergic to pine trees," he says. "Ever since I was a little kid."

Now I am really annoyed. He is surely one of those people in favor of shaving the rainforest right off of the world.

As if he is reading my thoughts, he says, "You know, I don't think there are pine trees in the rainforest. Too tropical."

Right there is where I shoot him. He falls on the newly installed Bloomingdale's carpet, blood spreading across his suit like a disaster map. I hold my nose and fish into his pocket for his cell phone.

I wonder for a moment why his wife is number 4. Who are the three ahead of her? I wonder if I'm one of them.

When his wife answers, I can tell by her voice she's in the middle of a manicure.

"You know," I say, losing my patience, "if you weren't so busy with your goddamn nails, you could have been number 1."

STUART DYBEK

FANTASY

"Do you fantasize about me?" she asked.

"Sure," he said, not volunteering any more information.

"I have the oddest fantasies about what I'd like to do with you," she said.

"Like what, for instance?"

"I want to shave you."

"I want to shave you too," he said.

"Not that way," she said. "I mean it. I picture you soaking in a steamy tub, a beautiful old claw footer, and I lather your beard with a boar-bristle brush. I even know where they sell them—at Crabtree & Evelyn. Then, you lie back and close your eyes, and with an old-fashioned straight razor that makes the sexiest scraping sound, I give you the best, closest shave you'll ever have.. Shave you clean and smooth and rinse your skin as if I'm your geisha."

"Sounds nice," he said, rather than tell her there was no way in hell she was getting near him with a razor.

Roberto G. Fernández

Wrong Channel

Barbarita stared out the window of her Miami apartment. Beads of sweat dripped from her eyebrows into her third cup of cold syrupy espresso. She was headed for the toilet when she heard the rattling sounds of Mima's old Impala.

"About time you got here," yelled Barbarita.

"It wouldn't start this morning."

Barbarita got in, tilted the rearview mirror, and applied enough rouge to her face for a healthier look. She wanted to make a good impression on the doctor who would approve her medical records for her green card. On the way to Jackson Memorial, Mima talked about her grandchildren.

Barbarita knocked a Bible and two *Reader's Digests* off the table when the nurse finally called her name.

"Sorry, ma'am, but you can't come in," the nurse said to Mima.

"I'm her interpreter," replied the polyglot.

"No bueno," said the doctor grimly as he walked in with Barbarita's X-rays. He told Mima, "Ask her if she had TB."

Mima turned to Barbarita. "He says, if you have a television?"

"Tell him yes, but in Havana. Not in Miami. But my daughter has a television here."

Mima told the doctor, "She says she had TV in Cuba, not in Miami, but her daughter has TV here."

"In that case we need to test her daughter for TB too."

Mima translated, "He says he needs to test your daughter's television to make sure it works, otherwise you cannot get your green card."

"Why the television?" asked a puzzled Barbarita.

"How many times did I tell you you needed to buy one? Don't you know, Barbarita? This is America."

KIM ADDONIZIO

BUT

They'd known each other a month and had decided to marry, but two days before the wedding she hit him over the head with a beer bottle during an argument and the paramedics had to come and he got sixteen stitches but what the hell, they reconciled as soon as they were sober. And then the wedding, a party in the warehouse space he lived in, and everyone still drinking and dancing as they headed off to a big hotel in the city. But the friend who was going to loan them a Lincoln to arrive in style never showed up, so they took the groom's old car and pulled up and staggered into the lobby, but with his bandaged head and the two of them being pretty wasted and some kind of complication about the name on the credit card--another friend had arranged for the room—the hotel refused to let them register. So back to his car, the old car that had no passenger window and now wouldn't start. He tried to hotwire it but somehow pulled out the ignition wire instead. After a while he got the car going but it had started to rain, hard, and they had to drive back home with her getting soaked and him holding one hand out the window to help the wiper blade sweep back and forth. At home the party was still going but by now the two of them wanted to be alone, and a nasty argument broke out between the groom and a few revelers who didn't want to leave, but finally they did and the newlyweds went to sleep after the bride threw up in a hand-painted ceramic pasta bowl someone had given them. In the morning they made love and things seemed better but when she got out of bed to pee she stepped on a piece of glass from a broken bottle, maybe the one she'd broken over his head the other night or maybe one of the several that had been broken the night before, and it was back to calling the ambulance and now no one has seen them for three days but they're probably fine, just holed up together in marital bliss, not killing each other with one of the guns he keeps, sometimes things start out badly but get better, by now they're surely better, they couldn't possibly screw things up any further but maybe they could.

Nick Hoppe

How to Waste Two Hours of Life

Bill Gillis closed his eyes. I'm so ashamed, he thought. I hate myself. I feel dirty, I feel used. I don't have a shred of self-esteem left in my body.

He had just watched "The Bachelorette" on television.

Bill could only blame himself, although it was his 30-year-old daughter Lisa, home for a few weeks after four years in Brazil and New York, who convinced him to do it. It was a bonding moment, he figured, but bonding was clearly overrated.

They were home alone, Bill's wife out of town. The Giants were on Comcast SportsNet, and real men were probably watching baseball. But Bill had made Lisa watch Matt Cain's perfect game last week, so it was her turn to choose.

She's hooked on "The Bachelorette," as are millions of other Americans, including Bill's other daughter. God help America, he thought.

He was only planning to watch until the first commercial, just to show Lisa he cared about her obsessions. He had lots of other options, including reading, going to the other television to watch the Giants, or perhaps jumping from the Golden Gate Bridge. Any of those might have been a better choice.

But "The Bachelorette," whose name was Emily, was kind of cute. And the eight remaining bachelors were some of the most handsome dweebs Bill had ever seen. As an added inducement, the scenery in Croatia, where they had gone to find true love, was spectacular.

Watching "The Bachelorette" was like gawking at a car accident on the freeway. Bill wanted to look away, but couldn't. He witnessed one awkward moment after another, and cringed and cringed, but he kept looking.

"There's no way she's going to end up with Travis," he told his daughter before he knew what he was saying. "There's absolutely no chemistry."

Travis had just gone on his one-on-one date with Emily. It went poorly, both for him and for Bill, who was saying things a real man shouldn't.

"She's going to end up with Arie, the race car driver," replied Lisa, slyly noting that Bill hadn't left after the first commercial, except to procure a beer for courage. "Some of my friends think Sean is the one, but I don't."

Bill was getting them all confused, but by the third commercial he had it down. He agreed the best bets were Arie and Sean, and maybe Jeff had a chance. He also felt sick.

Meanwhile, Emily was dating them all, taking them to sights in Croatia and talking about love and marriage and ending up each date with a lot of kissing.

"THAT SLUT!" Bill cried after she locked lips with the sixth bachelor in the last five minutes. "She doesn't even like Doug! How can she kiss him? Yuck!"

Then she dumped Travis, denying him "a rose." And Travis started to cry.

"ARE YOU KIDDING ME?" Bill screamed. "He's been on two dates with Emily! Please don't cry, Travis," he pleaded. "You're an embarrassment to mankind."

"He really liked her," Lisa said, although he could tell she was cringing as well. "But he does seem a bit sensitive."

At this point, Bill was mesmerized by the awkwardness of the show. Commercials flew by. He looked at his watch as he got another beer. He had wasted an hour and a half of his life, with half an hour to go.

Bill could feel the dirt clinging to his body. He wanted to take a shower. Instead, he told his daughter she should have a party where everyone sits around watching "The Bachelorette" and drinks a shot of tequila every time someone on the show says the word "amazing."

"It's been done," she replied. "Not many people make it through the first hour."

The train wreck was coming to the end of its episode, and Bill couldn't turn away. It was one "amazing" and/or "awesome" encounter after another. Emily and Arie were clearly bonding, but she had feelings for all the little nerds. Her heart was confused, and if she had a brain, it might have been confused as well.

Finally, mercifully, it was over. Scenes from next week's episode of "The Bachelorette" filled the screen. There was going to be trouble with Arie and Emily, who seemed so right for each other. What a surprise.

No way I'll be watching, Bill thought. But I'll be secretly rooting for Sean. He's my favorite. Emily doesn't deserve him.

Kirk Nesset

Believing in People

I'm at the new super, shopping. The aisles are luxury freeways. The linoleum glows with a force like belief. I glide along with my bright steel basket. Up comes this guy, pale, bone-skinny, not altogether bad looking, saying Hey, can you help me?

Depends, I say, looking up from my cart.

Pretend you're my girlfriend, he says. Just for a minute—I'll pay for your groceries.

He's got the cheekbones and cheeks, albeit pockmarked; the solid black eyes, the inward stare. The mole on the chin.

His ex chick's over in produce, he says. He can't stand thinking she's thinking he's single, i.e., muddled, bitter, lonely, unhinged. Do I know the feeling? Will I play along for his sake, for the price of the beer in my basket, the diet colas, tortillas, mozzarella, tomatoes, potatoes, green onions, V-8 and milk?

I'm not done shopping, I tell him.

He looks around and says, Buy what you want. His lip trembles, almost. His hand does for sure. He's no scammer. I do know the feeling. He wears cologne you can trust.

Okay, I say.

He asks me my name. I tell him Danielle. A clerk slides by, mustachioed, muscled, feather duster pluming from hind pocket.

Danielle what?

Just Danielle.

We roll past the pasta and gourmet food section, the frozen foods, vitamins, toothpaste and shampoo, heading for produce. At the bulk coffee bins I withdraw a bag, press a lever; oil-slick beans flutter in. My mock-love hovers by Tortilla Chip Mountain at the end of the row, surveilling. Muzak hangs in the fluorescent air.

There, at the meat counter—she's shuffling fresh chicken breasts.

Average-looking, she is. Average brown hair, average brown eyes, average understated hips and flat butt. Not that I'm unaverage myself. I spend more time at the gym, keep my tan up, and had a tit-job, is all.

Chuck the ex says hello to Miss Average. The chick checks me out. I smile my manic ditz smile.

Lisa, this is Danielle, Chuck says.

Lisa and I say hi. Chuck asks how has she been. I stand there acting girlfriend-like, mock-awkward. A beef tongue lolls below my left elbow, swelling against its plastic wrap. A few feet down is the tank of live lobsters. Extraterrestrial things. Armored. Foot-long feelers jutting out at the head.

Where do you work, Danielle? Lisa says.

Nowhere, I lie. I just lay around, like, and sulk.

Chuck nods, grinning, mock-knowing. Lisa asks what do I do when I do work. I model, I lie. Oh, she says. A voice wafts down from speakers somewhere. Change, please, register six.

By now we're up even with the lobster tank. A pair have squared off, raising their Japanese-horror-flick claws—cudgels, not pinchers, clamped with black rubber bands.

Chuck says you pack a punch in the sack, I say to Lisa.

Chuck's eyes bug out a little but he keeps his composure.

Whatever he says, says Lisa, flushing. He's the expert.

I wouldn't call him that.

No, I guess I wouldn't either, she answers.

A Chinese family floats by on the right, short shiny-haired parents, shiny amber-faced kids. Chuck's hands are shaking; his jowls have gone pink. He speaks.

Well, I guess—

Don't worry, I tell his ex. I made him confess. I wouldn't let up. But God, I say, shaking my head. He made a religion of you.

Chuck leans on the counter, trembling, inspecting cellophaned fish. Halibut, turbot, snapper, mahi-mahi filets. Lobsters clunk in the tank.

You ended his innocence, I say, stroking Chuck's arm hairs. Most of it, anyway. Somebody had to. This is the twenty-first century.

I don't even know this woman, Chuck says.

Me, I say, I cracked years ago. Everything gone in a puff. Love. Youth. You name it. Weird thing is, the guys I end up with are always where he is. You know, on the verge. Ready to lose that last little ounce.

What do you mean you don't know her, Lisa asks Chuck.

Price check on four, the loudspeaker says.

Chuck begins but I cut him off. I kiss him. He backs toward the lobsters. I shove my tongue in his mouth, angle my hips into his.

Jesus, Lisa says, pushing away.

He's stronger than he looks but I'm stronger still, I keep him pinned. Water slaps in the tank. Shoppers roll by behind us. The butcher gapes from a doorway, stains on his apron.

Listen, I'll say, when I finally release him. Believing in people will kill you. Take it from me.

Meg Pokrass

Divorced Devout's Potluck

We meet at a Divorced Devout's potluck. He is as cute as Jesus would have been after playing racquetball. Sweaty and ropey, smiling like a choirboy. This week I joined the group . . . a big step. I've decided to shove it all, to get out . . . live life . . . before I'm off to the big, luxury condo in the sky. Confessions get old.

I sit on the same side of the picnic table as him, that first day. He has Jesus-blond hair, short and bird-fluffy.

How many men have I kissed right here in this very spot over the last forty years? One. Morris, who left me for an atheist waitress at Hooters. Now I am a middle-aged sinner, with real breasts that feel floppy.

He says his name is Goliath, but I already know it's a wonderful lie.

I fidget a bit, beat my foot to an old John Denver song—"Sunshine on my shoulders makes me happy . . ."—and continuously look around behind me as if we are being stalked by Lucifer.

There is an enormous sadness radiating from him. I want to gather him, break his bread and let it melt in my mouth. I want to make him forget his ex. I am wearing heels and stockings, a short yellow dress that hugs my body. I adore men of a certain type—this type. He is Jesus plus Meatloaf meets The Little Prince. Shorts, white T-shirt, potbelly peeking out. . . a sexy rock star curl to his lip. I'm a townie. I'm a lonely woman with a great love of unique potholders. I already want him.

I slide my face up close beside Goliath's cheek and say, *What's that scent?* It hardly matters what he answers—he turns his head and gives me his business card. A-Promise Insurance, Bill Bithers, four phone numbers and three e-mail addresses. His eyelids are soft and sweet. Though he sells insurance, I am undaunted.

The next night I go to his houseboat. He's invited me for celery and dip.

He no longer has the same, fluffy hair. Now he's as butch as the devil himself. Athletic, creamy generous pectorals, unexpectedly vulnerable against his sea captain tan. He is dominant; he will always be dominant. My Goliath.

We share a bottle and a half of Chianti, sitting on the deck of his houseboat, watching the twinkling island of Alcatraz.

Later, on his captain's cot, he moves against me like gently lapping water. I kiss his chin and taste celery dip. I slither my hand over his rock candy mountain. He playfully pushes my hand away. We are halfway to hell in a spinning teacup, because this is a game, we both know what is happening here. He is here . . . I am here . . . we are divorced and unholy and I'm as moist and perky as a peasant.

I won't break the good china, he says. Nothing makes sense, which is fine.

Soft sleek digging hard moaning wide with want; my singing mouth is next to his deaf ear.

Is this nice? Is this what you like? Divorce has done its damage.

It's VERY OKAY!

I beg him to thrust his giant-killing club into my dragon's lair. He nods, kneels on the bed and skips into me with his staff, holds me like that for so long I can't wait for the songbook. I grab feverishly for his invisible hair with my hands. He is a giant killer!

He pushes and I am gasping full arched bodyless mindless somewhere else entirely. He rides the Christmas of me with his bishop. He puts his mouth on my lady lily . . . .

He has always been here and will always be here, keeping me on this exquisite edge.

When I finally give it up, it is with a sob of relief and prayer.

We lie in a tangle of non-alcoholic punch and limbs. He tastes like rummage sales and Christmas bake-offs in the best way possible.

In the middle of the night, we wake to the sound of a foghorn or a text tone. Once more, his meaty knish is instantly happier in my velvet donation box. When I sing *Hallelujah* he says to bring it down a bit, there are dogs in the neighboring houseboats.

The ending is already written into the beginning. We are fated to ride to hell on The Cyclone.

I drive home before dawn, catch the end of "The Trouble With Angels" on AMC. Before falling asleep, I give the cats a few treats. They have never seemed more ravenous.

John Haggerty

Outside the Box

"Aaaaarrrggh!"

"Aaarrgh?"

"Yeah, but with more of a kind of guttural thing in the middle. Aaaaarrrggh!"

"What does it mean?"

"Uh . . . well, you know. 'I want to feast on the flesh of the living!' Or something."

"Jesus. You have two months to come up with a campaign, and you bring me this? Christ, how about 'Flesh! It's fresh!' or 'The human meat I want to eat!' I mean, I'm just spitballing here, just throwing stuff out and it's better than 'Aaargh.'"

"More like 'Aaaaarrrggh!' You know. Kind of raspy."

"That's not the fucking point. The point is that some weird moan is not an advertising tag line. 'Warm meat! Let's eat!' Now that is an advertising tag line."

"Tremendous stuff, Rob. Brilliant. We really lost a major talent when they kicked you upstairs. But here's the thing: we don't actually know if they understand English anymore. And to be honest . . ."

"What? Spit it out."

"Well, some of us are wondering if this is a market segment we should pursue."

"Are you crazy? Have you seen the numbers? I have spreadsheets that will blow your minds. The Post-Living market is just exploding. It is the single fastest-growing demographic in the country right now. And you're telling me that you don't want to pursue it?"

"Well, first there is the ethical . . ."

"Gray area. It's a gray area."

"Yes, the idea of selling human flesh to zombies is something of a gray area ethically. But beyond that, we just don't know very much about them. They don't seem to spend money or engage in leisure activities. They aren't interested in sex at all, and that takes a lot of bullets out of the gun, marketing-wise. Aside from an obvious attraction to eating . . . uh, the rest of us, we really don't know how to incentivize them. And so far, the focus groups have not gone well. Very, very badly, in fact."

"Bullshit. You're all on a fucking failure safari here. Let me bottom line it for you: I want this. It's the most exciting emerging market I have ever seen. We are going to own it. And this team is going to find a way or you're going to find new jobs. Thomson! You've been awfully quiet today. You're the executive on this account. Any sage words?"

"Sorry Rob. It's just that . . . well, my wife, uh, transitioned last night."

"She transitioned! Thomson, that is excellent news!"

"Not really. She, well . . ."

"No, don't you see? You've got an in! You've got a courtside seat at the hottest game in town. This changes everything. I want you get inside her head. Find out what makes her tick."

"Well, that's the thing. She . . . she attacked my son, and there was a bit of a struggle, and I had to pin her up against the wall with a chair while my son hit her with a baseball bat. And she just wouldn't quit, and he hit her and hit her. And her head flattened on the side that he was hitting her but she was still so strong, and I think some of her brains got in my hair and there was this terrible smell of rotting flesh and fresh blood. And then the chair shattered and she grabbed my son and was slowly pulling him toward her mouth, except that half of her jaw was gone and she couldn't really get a good bite. Finally I took the leg of the broken chair, and I drove it through her shattered skull and held her like that, and my son brought the sledgehammer from the basement and I pinned her there, impaled my wife against the dining room wall, and I think she's still there. I mean, I really, really hope she's still there, because otherwise I don't know where she would be, and that would be so much worse . . ."

"Is she dead?"

"Oh, God, I hope so. But they kind of start out that way, so it's hard to tell for sure."

"Damn! That's a missed opportunity. Well, did she say anything?"

"Just sort of made noises. 'Mmmmurrggh.' Like that."

"Mmmmurgh?"

"Mmmmuuuuugrrgh!"

"Nice. That's actually got a really nice feel to it. Mmmmuuurrgrgrgrrgh!"

"Mmmmmmmmuuuuuurggh! That's great, Rob. You have a real talent for getting outside the box."

"Mmmmmuuuuuuuugrgrggh! I love it. It's got kind of a hip-hop feel, doesn't it? Gentlemen, call the art department. They will be working late tonight. We are going to eat this market alive."

Tori Bond

Swimming with the Chickens

Those golden-roasted chickens were feisty swimmers. I complained to the lifeguard that dinner did not belong in the pool with my kid.

"Someone might drown."

A glaze of teenage condescension closed over the lifeguard's eyes. His chest puffed up like a hairless life vest inflated with absolute power over the pool population.

"No one likes a tattle-tale at any age, sir."

Five deliciously caramelized hens dunked my daughter when she exited the frog tongue slide. I had to beat them off with a metal barbecue fork. I got scolded for doing harm to those animals that tried wrestling my daughter to a watery death. Katie and I were forced to sit poolside on our towels for a time-out because of my savagery, but those nasty, mouth-watering chickens went unpunished.

"Bullies, that's what they are," I growled to my daughter. "Just because they're small and beakless doesn't mean they're not dangerous." The lifeguards mistakenly thought they were charming, with their crispy skin and irresistible juiciness.

"They're so cunning," I said, working myself into a foaming-at-the-mouth frenzy. "They're too smart to show their pack mentality in front of anyone with authority." Katie inched away from me to dangle her hand in the cool grease-slicked water.

This is what I got for wanting a better life for us, living in one of the better vegan neighborhoods. Don't get me wrong, vegans are good people, but they let those damn chickens get away with murder in the name of humanitarianism. I hated those bullies, they made me want to tear their limbs off and shred their tender nuggets with my canines. But I controlled my animal urges—I didn't want my daughter to suffer because her father was an outed carnivore. The schools here were worth biting my tongue for. I chomped on a carrot stick, watching the flock frolic in the kiddy pool while we roasted in the sun waiting to be released from our injustice.

Charles Rafferty

My Yoga Pants, My Executioner

You laugh, but I was once the most sought-after male yoga pants model in the world—not just Rhode Island, not just the Eastern seaboard. The world.

It was back in the 80s, when yoga pants were first catching fire. I was the go-to model for solids. True, I'm a little flabby now, but I was a god back then—like Michelangelo's David dipped into ink or azure sky or the yellow tongue of a candle's flame. They gave the leopard prints and camouflage to the models with stubby legs and ankles full of spider veins. To everyone else, is what I mean.

Jacques was my rival and my downfall. He was the French male yoga pants model, and everyone fell in love with his clove cigarettes, the pretentious way he had of going by just his first name—like he was Cher or Twiggy.

Let's face it. It was a woman's world. The yoga pants catalogues rarely needed more than one male model. Oh, we did some shoots together—Jacques and I. But the money was always looking for something vaguely homoerotic. They were pushing the envelope, and it's one of the reasons that even today the yoga pants industry is seen as a pioneer in gay friendliness.

Anyway, I couldn't pull it off. I remember the exact moment things went bad, and I felt my career turning like a ship toward the reef that had always been there. Jacques was doing the downward dog at sunset on a beach in Bora Bora. We'd waited all afternoon for the light to be right, and then they passed me a bottle of Bain de Soleil and told me to rub it into his back. Jacques was hairy. Too hairy. All the French male models acted like they'd never heard of waxing. It was revolting to have my fingers on him. I ended up looking like someone who had walked in on a dissection, or like I'd been given a live cricket to eat. The light changed. The shoot was ruined. And I flew home to a phone that never rang again.

Jacques rode the craze for all he was worth, and I won't begrudge him that. I had lived at the very core of the yoga pants world, and understood its fierce allure—the private jets, the champagne breakfasts, the pedicures, the endless sea of women reaching for a touch. But it was work, too. On the yoga pants circuit, life was an endless schedule of squats and treadmills, tofu and grapefruit juice.

Then Richard Simmons got popular, and the bottom fell out. Everyone wanted baggy striped shorts, which in my opinion are just too forgiving. He was essentially promoting being out of shape. It was a lazy man's fitness.

Although I couldn't get work, I still had my money. But I was too young to handle it. My father was a banker and I could have used his advice, but we were on the outs back then. He had wanted a son who played football or who joined the Marines—not a son who rocked the camera in yoga pants. So I was left with the advice of the only people I trusted—my stylist and my whole-foods consultant. Unfortunately, they said to put the money into Swatches and leg warmers. And I did. But I bought high, and had to sell low. It's an old story.

I don't even wear yoga pants anymore. Too many memories. Too many ghosts. I went through a period of heavy drinking, but eventually I picked myself up, went back to college, and took my degree in marine science. In fact, I'm packing for a trip right now to study the turtles of Bora Bora. I'd be lying if I didn't admit to some misgivings. Returning to those beaches after all these years will be a lot like the soldiers going back to Normandy, I imagine. It's going to hurt, but I feel like I'm ready (fingers crossed).

As for Jacques, I heard he overdosed at a Boy George after-party. This was during the comeback tour. They found him facedown and shirtless beside his works, wearing a pair of motley stirrup pants. He still didn't believe in waxing, and stirrup pants—for god's sake—should only be worn as solids.

Jacques, oh Jacques! Even I never hoped you would fall so far.

KONA MORRIS

I'M PRETTY SURE NICOLAS CAGE IS MY GYNECOLOGIST

I really am. His nose is a little different, but it's probably one of those prosthetic molds they use for the movies, so he can get away with it. He's got the exact head shape, smooth vampire hair, intense eyes, scrunched eyebrow wrinkles, large-lipped open mouth. His height, body, and posture are all spot-on—the hunched forward shoulders, long gangly arms. And I would know that voice anywhere, always sounding like there's a yawn trapped behind it waiting to come out. Only, instead of saying, "I came here to drink myself to death," he says, "All right, just relax back. Oh yes, this is a very healthy looking vagina. Okay, now I'm going to put my fingers on you. Do they feel cold? Okay, now I'm going to insert them." It's very nerve-racking to have Nicolas Cage's fingers inside me.

Every once in a while during the preliminary exam, he has a burst of spastic energy that causes him to launch across the room and intensely run his hand through his hair. When he's a gynecologist, he behaves a lot more like he did in his old films. There's a sweet crack in his voice, a criminal twinkle in his eyes, and his movements are enchanting as they shift from energetic spasms to sedated and slouching.

I imagine I'm Kathleen Turner in *Peggy Sue Got Married* and he's pacing back and forth in my parents' basement. "Look, I've got the hair. I've got the teeth. I've got the eyes. Peggy, look outside that window. I've got the car. I'm the lead singer. I'm the man." He is convincing and I almost fall for him, but then I realize he is actually flipping through my chart and asking me what kind of birth control I use. I can hardly answer I'm so distracted by his presence. I want to tell him I'm barren, a rocky place where his seed can find no purchase. I want him to do impossibly sweet things for me like climb up ladders and steal babies.

There's a hint of frozen sadness in his expression, something gray in the skin and frightened behind his eyes. I wonder if it's because of all the horrible movies he's done in the last ten years and how obvious it is that they were just for the money. I want to hug him and tell him it's okay—that he redeemed himself in *Bad Lieutenant: Port of Call New Orleans*. That we can forget about *Ghost Rider* now and move on.

When he's got his two fingers pressing against my fallopian tubes, his eyebrows say it all. They shift smoothly, the skin in-between them rising and falling. His face tilts slightly to one side and his lower lip drops down, pausing in that second before speech in the way only he can, holding it still for what feels forever, or at least a pregnant pause.

His eyes are soft and shining as they look at me over my spread, gown-covered legs. They make me giggle because of their sincerity. This causes awkwardness for him, like he is suddenly aware that I know who he is, the façade of being a doctor has vanished, and now he is just a famous actor with his fingers deep inside a random woman's vaginal cavity. He diverts his vision, pulls out, and slaps his latex glove off and into the trash in one fell swoop with a quick hop to the other side of the room. He starts to mumble, shuffle, and stutter, "I . . . I . . . I have to go grab the speculum." His tone is mysterious and breathy, with hints of unnecessary apology, like the self-conscious Charlie Kaufman in *Adaptation*.

When he comes back he has collected himself, but he is rushing. He no longer makes eye contact with me. He seems anxious, like when he woke from the dream about how he had unleashed the lone biker of the apocalypse after Florence Arizona found her little Nathan gone, but he dives back in anyway. He jams the tool far up inside and clicks it shut on the nose end of my cervix. It's pinching and burning as he uses the long, slender swab to collect enough slime to test. I try to say something to show him that I'm okay with who he is, that I don't need a real gynecologist, an actor is fine with me, but then he is gone, taking my pap smear with him.

Shelby Raebeck

My Hypoglycemic Son and ADD Wife

I

"Suzy, did Lucas have Lucky Charms again for breakfast?"

"Yes, darling. And a whole bagel with Nutella—he just loves Nutella!"

"Well, you better go next door. I think he's scaring the dachshund."

"Oh, he *loves* that puppy. Is he growling through the fence again?"

"Suzy, I'm home. Picked up some whole grain pasta for dinner."

"One step ahead of you, sweetheart. Just fed Lucas a huge tin of mac and cheese from the deli. He devoured it."

"Remember, honey, regular pasta gets metabolized into sugar. And we're supposed to go easy on the dairy."

"It's just one meal, darling. And look at how happy he is running up and down the block."

"What's that he's wearing?"

"A camouflage cape! He tore down the curtains in his room and then rolled in the mud. Isn't he *something*?"

II

"Honey, please feed Lucas Cheerios and soy milk for breakfast and don't pack more than one juice box for lunch."

"Don't worry about lunch, dear. The third grade is going to Chuck E. Cheese's after school so we'll have a big meal there. He never eats his lunch anyway. Good thing he drinks his juice boxes."

"Try to go easy on the pizza and ice cream. Remember what happened at the birthday party?"

"Oh, the whole camera episode in the bowling alley bathroom? Those boys were so naughty! I'll make sure he eats a full lunch. And I'll bring juice boxes for the ride!"

"I'm home, honey. How'd it go today?"

"Today?"

"At Chuck E. Cheese's."

"Why're you asking me?"

"Is everything okay? Where's Lucas?"

"Down in the den."

"Suzy, what's going on? He's down there playing Grand Theft Auto online with some pharmacist in Tulsa."

"I gave him a credit card. It was the only thing that would shut him up."

"What happened?"

"Chuck E. Cheese's had their Wednesday special—pizza and the ice cream sundae buffet. The kids had a blast, eating and just pounding away at that Whac-A-Mole. We could only get them to leave by luring them to the car with Red Bull. On the way home I got pulled over by a cop who saw Lucas peeing out the window."

"Red Bull, Suzy? Do you not listen to anything I say?"

"I certainly didn't hear the part about him going Oedipal."

"He was just peeing."

"When we got home, I told him to go to his room, and he tore off his clothes and raced out of the house stark naked, screaming, 'My Mommy's trying to rape me! My mommy's trying to rape me!'"

"Perhaps you regret the Red Bull?"

"This woman from social services showed up. First, she questioned him, then it was my turn, and to keep him occupied, I gave him a box of Oreos and sent him into the den to play Call of Duty."

"Oh, that'll keep his attention."

"Not anymore. After the woman left, I went down and told him 'duty' means following orders, obeying the rules. He tried to ignore me so I stood in front of the screen and read the video's disclaimer about all action in the game being in accordance with the Geneva Convention. He yanked out the disk, said it was 'Pussy Duty,' and smashed it on the floor."

III

"Suzy, I went ahead this morning and cooked breakfast."

"You expect him to eat that?"

"I added some salt and maple syrup. Lucas! Lucas! Oh, good morning, buddy."

"What's this, ostrich shit?"

"Oatmeal. Try it."

"Try this."

"Maybe with a little more syrup . . ."

"Keep pouring, mister."

"Let go of my hand, Lucas!"

"Oooh, syrupy ostrich shit."

"Time to go to school, sweetie. Don't forget your lunch."

"Energy bars?"

"Three, darling. And a brand new energy drink."

"Good—I am way over juice boxes. At lunchtime, I been walking over to Starbucks with the eighth graders. They buy me Venti Frappuccinos then dare me to do shit."

Arthur Hoppe

The Waiting Game

"Good afternoon. May I help you?"

"Yes, I'm Dr. Herbert Vamplew and I'm here to see a patient, Fred Frisbee, for his annual checkup."

"Oh, yes, I'm Mrs. Frisbee. Do you have an appointment, Doctor?"

"Yes, for one o'clock. I'm a few minutes early, I'm afraid."

"That's quite all right. Please have a seat in the living room and patient will be with you as soon as possible."

"Thank you. Excuse me, who are those other gentlemen in there?"

"Oh, that's Dr. Katz, Dr. Trevis and Dr. Clagenson. Patient feels you can't be too careful and he wants a second, third and fourth opinion. While you're waiting, will you please fill out this medical history form?"

"My medical history?"

"Yes, it asks where you attended medical school, what courses you took, honors, if any, and your financial assets in case of a malpractice suit. Then you might wish to browse through this copy of *Look* magazine. There's an interesting article predicting victory for Barry Goldwater."

"Mrs. Frisbee? Remember me, Mrs. Frisbee? I'm Dr. Vamplew and I've now been waiting an hour and a half to see the patient."

"Oh, we haven't forgotten you, Doctor. Patient is running a little late today. He got stuck in a sand trap on the 17th."

"Look here! I'm a very busy man and. . ."

"Of course you are. But patient is with a doctor right now."

"How many doctors are ahead of me?"

"I do think maybe you're next. Why don't you follow me out here to this powder room? After I close the door, please remove your coat and put on this white medical jacket with the opening on the front and have a seat. Here's a copy of *War and Peace* to keep you occupied. I'm sure patient will be with you at any minute."

"Mrs. Frisbee, I've been in that powder room two hours and I'm not waiting another minute!"

"Oh, there you are, Dr. Vamplew. I was wondering where I put you. I'm so sorry, but patient was called away on an emergency. They needed a fourth for dominoes. But let's make another appointment, shall we? Let's see, patient can see you at 2 P.M. seven weeks from next Tuesday. How does that sound, doctor? Doctor? Doctor! Darn, now we'll need another new front door. These doctors just don't seem to understand how valuable a patient's time is these days."

Gail Louise Siegel

Author Interview

Who are your major influences?

Hilda Gillespie, ever since I saw her at MLA—a party where she wore this green sweater that matched her eyes? So I applied to her master class and kind of quit my job at J. Walter Thompson and followed her around from workshop to workshop until she recognized me. I kept submitting basically the same story but I'd change the main character's name from Betsy to Maude to Shunice. And where she was from. She started out in Toledo but she was from Watts by the time I got to Sewanee. Anyway, I bought Hilda a drink to apologize, and one thing led to another. Maybe she didn't like my writing, but it was pretty well known that she'd sleep with anyone after four drinks. So afterward, we emailed, and I read her novels, and I think—maybe so I wouldn't call or text her husband—she told me to submit the Betsy/Maude/Shunice story to *Ploughshares*, and the rest is, well, history.

Do you write on paper or a computer?

Funny you should ask, because yesterday I was looking for a black pen to sign my taxes, and there wasn't a single black pen in the house. Every damn pen had blue ink: marine, turquoise, peacock. Now, why is that? But, paper or computer. I grew up with typewriters. I had this five-ton Selectric with a correcting ribbon. It erased automagically but it wasn't portable. I wrote *Paper Vampire* in composition books at Mespresso, this great place to eavesdrop. Eavesdropping really helps with dialogue. Anyway, the covers were brown or pink cardboard, whatever I could steal from my father's office supply inventory. Maybe that's why the rape scene happens in a stationery shop. Now I have a laptop. Still, I'll write on anything—a napkin, an envelope, a legal pad, a receipt. I record notes on my iPhone. Be careful with that, though. I had this party where I put the iPhone in the music dock and right after Lucinda Williams, I was uncorking the wine and this woman started reciting a poem about her cervical exam--but it was actually a 'note-to-self' and boy, I hit that fast forward button so quick I spilled the malbec all over my boyfriend.

What made you start writing?

Maybe you heard that my sister and I were shipped off to boarding school? It was this old stone complex in the middle of a poison ivy farm. They were probably breeding it for chemical warfare. And there were no phone calls allowed. I hated it, especially the big square group shower house when you soaped up with twenty girls, nozzles on the perimeter, everybody watching to see who'd grown pubes. Gretchen didn't mind so much, but still, we had a kind of contest, in our letters home, to see who could make mom come get us. We wrote reams of paper, and I had this flair for describing the bats, bugs in the food, etc. Gretch said I lied, but it's not lying, it's, you know, emphasizing the enforced nudity, the dungeon and the manacles. Embellishing, maybe. I read lots of Dickens. But I swear I did not contact that reporter and my quotes in her so-called exposé were exaggerated. It didn't go to trial, and Gretchen and I didn't even go home early.

What's Your Favorite Color?

Now, that's a loaded question. When I was little, it was red, of course. I'm passionate and fiery and even in junior high, I was interested in vampires. But then in high school our rival's school colors were red and white, and their mascot was an Indian. How racist. Plus, my boyfriend was Indian. Not that kind, with the headdress. The other kind. Manjit's family had this big sari palace with reams of sparkly fabric, and he turned me on to imported cotton and colors like tangerine and melon. So I gave up red. Then at college it was maize and blue everywhere—and even though I wasn't into football I had this real appreciation for food-related colors from Manjit. Call it nostalgia. So it was maize for years until the gypsy on Maxwell Street did my chart and said that purple was best for my karma and my hair, too. Sometimes I still miss Manjit, but that little bitch from Delhi with the Ph.D. who his parents got him to marry? Always wore purple. Anyway, since then I've started highlighting my hair so, maybe lilac. Or red.

STEVEN GRAY

HANSEL AND GRETEL IN CALIFORNIA

Once upon a time there was an old woman who would kill teenagers and eat them. She lived in Marin County and her home was covered with marijuana plants. When high school students came up to her house in the woods to score some weed she would invite them in, get them stoned, and when they were so high they couldn't see straight, push them into the oven. Considering they were full of THC it was like making pot brownies, except it was baked high school students.

One day a boy and girl were walking by after school and noticed the pot plants all over the house. They walked up and were pulling off leaves when the old bat invited them in for a smoke. The girl was suspicious; she was an honors student who wanted to be a nurse and this didn't seem quite copacetic. Her boyfriend was a lowlife, but she put up with him because psycho-sexually she needed to feel like she was slumming in bed or she couldn't come. But that's another story. While her boyfriend was getting ripped with the crone, she only pretended to inhale. She wandered around the place, and glancing out a grimy back window she saw a skeleton in the hot tub wearing a baseball cap with the name of her high school on it. Math was her specialty, so she put 2 + 2 together and came up with: homicidal stoner cannibal witch. She pretended she was wasted, slowing down her reaction time and not finishing sentences. When the old woman grabbed Hansel's belt and led him to the oven where she dried her dope, Gretel realized the crone meant to perform a Hanselectomy on the world. Gretel had spent too much time on the behavioral modification of her stoner boyfriend to lose him now, so she was only protecting her investment when she shoved the cackling cannibal into the oven, slammed the door, and cooked her goose.

"Dude, that's elder abuse!" the boyfriend cried, and in fact the girl was arrested, but since she was a minor she only did eight months in juvie. The boyfriend consoled himself by smoking all the old bitch's bud and became permanently spaced out, so he moved to Bolinas.

Adam Johnson

Denti-Vision Satellite

In the oral surgery bay, Boyden prepares for the day's last patient. Boyden spreads the canal tools, then changes bits, test-whirring the drill. Across the chair, Cammy pulls a tray of explorers from the autoclave. She's wearing a necklace of ridiculous beads, a gift Boyden's given her. It's the wampum they'll use to buy drinks on the Club Med trip he's surprised her with. She wears them now, a run of colored fruits and molded seashells, as a badge of anger, that regardless of whether this is the second anniversary of Boyden's divorce, she's pissed he's not taking her to Switzerland.

Boyden's a finalist for the coveted Denti-Vision award, given each year in Geneva. The prize encourages ideas for bettering the industry. One proposal calls for shipping old equipment to the Third World, while another sends mercy dental teams to Canada. Boyden's idea is a new kind of root canal, a procedure in which porcelain-sleeved needles, acting as electrodes, are pushed into the jaw through the gums to electrically deaden the roots of molars. Boyden's calling it "Electrodontia," based on an idea he got from his ex-wife, Clorad, who loved electrolysis. Cammy calls her Clorox.

But there's a fourth finalist whose proposal is so brilliant that Boyden can't get it out of his head: it calls for the creation of an international, 24-hour, all-dental satellite that would broadcast pure dentistry, live, from 200 channels.

With the instruments out, Cammy starts heating the polymer.

"Just tell me why," she says.

"Why what?"

She points a spreader at him. "Give me one reason I can't go. If you love me, then there's a reason."

On the walls are outdated photos of his children, Philip and Claire: baby-toothed and cheeky, they don't know they're living at the horizon of their own family, that it's about to end.

"In Switzerland, you'll see me lose this award," he says. "You're not going to like me in Switzerland."

Boyden turns on the radio. He prefers a station that plays hits from the 60s and 70s, and he hums the lyrics of tunes like "White-Tipped Glove" and "Chocolate Factory" as he works, careful not to let his toes start tapping on the foot pedal.

Some days, when the music is right, the holes just drill themselves.

Boyden sets up his Sony-Cam to get tape for his presentation. Right now he needs footage of how painful "old fashioned" dentistry used to be before Electrodontia was invented. But when the patient comes in, Boyden remembers him as a laugher.

His name is Mr. Franks. At the sight of the yellow vinyl chair, Franks starts a giggle that never goes away. It is to be a straight root canal—drill, cut, file, melt, pack—though nothing today will be straight, Boyden realizes. Once in the chair, Franks clamps his hands onto his belt buckle as if it were a signal mirror, then snickers at everything from the Lidocaine needles to the endo files. Cammy installs the dental dam with a crisp snap.

Boyden flashes her one last smile, just to see if sex is out of the question.

That's what tends to happen after the last patient. They take turns reclining in the vinyl chair, and at their disposal are the air and water pistol, the saliva suction pump, the swing-arm grips—like pommel holds, those things. The number 7 nozzle is his favorite, and the Thompson L-handle Extruder, with the worm-drive extension, makes her speak in tongues. There's the pink numbing gel, the sonic gun, the rubber molding kit.

Right now, though, that feels a thousand miles away.

On the radio, The Tooth Fairies sing, "Wear My Sweater."

Boyden grinds down the cusps with a knurling bit, but when the smell of burning dentin hits the air, Mr. Franks begins a chocky, back-of-the-throat laugh that gives Boyden the creeps. Then Franks starts watching the procedure reflected in Boyden's glasses. It's like the guy is peering inside Boyden's soul, finding everything stupidly funny.

Boyden runs an explorer into the pulp—sending Franks' eyes wide.

"Doctor," Cammy gasps, but Boyden only grabs the drill.

He starts to think of that satellite, unblinking, hovering, always there. It's too perfect. This world doesn't deserve it. The day is a wash, the videotape unusable, forget Cammy, Clora, the kids. As Wayne and the Wax Museum thump the funky baseline to "Boog the Groove," Boyden's drill starts to wander in all that decay.

NANCY STOHLMAN

DONNY AND MARIE OSMOND BARBIE

My Donny and Marie Osmond Barbie dolls came with matching purple outfits—Donny had purple socks that slipped into white shoes, and both Donny and Marie had holes drilled through their left hands for their matching microphones that I promptly lost. Their brunette heads were fastened onto typical Barbie bodies, Marie's 38—22—26, feet permanently arched for high-heels, Donny's nondescript bulge.

There was only one game I played with Donny and Marie Osmond Barbie, who were no longer brother and sister. It went like this: Donny wakes one morning ready for another exciting day in plastic world. After a refreshing plastic breakfast, he decides to go to the mall. In the atrium of the mall an event is happening, a large, raised platform with a line of beautiful women, including Marie. It's a Wife Auction—the fast-talking announcer is rattling off his prizes to the highest bidder.

Now Donny really isn't in the market for a wife on this beautiful Saturday in plastic world, but he's never seen anyone as beautiful as Marie in his whole life. As one woman after another is bid on and married away to the mall-visiting man of her dreams, Donny can't stop looking at his Marie. He approaches the stage, starry-eyed. He bids. He wins.

Marie is shy, demure behind that perpetual toothy smile. Like any bride wife who has just been sold from a platform in the middle of a shopping mall, she is nervous. She approaches the edge of the stage as if she is entering civilization for the first time. She shyly accepts Donny's hand and steps from the platform, scared like a little bird. The few onlookers applaud the new married couple.

Donny, now manly and confident, leads his new wife away from the auctioning block, away from the platform and the mall to his shoebox Ferrari. A short drive across the carpet later the newlyweds arrive home. Marie is again overwhelmed, as she's apparently never seen a house before, and Donny shows her the two plastic fold-up walls ending at the bedroom, which, ironically, is the only room in this cheap, non-Barbie brand plastic house. In the fold-out plastic bed they kiss, him the sweet but firm aggressor, her compliant, and then finally they are naked, her plastic legs swiveled out, his nondescript bulge pushing between.

The plot never went any further. By then the game had reached its shaky conclusion, the sky was darkening and my mother was calling me to dinner.

Tom Hazuka

Sunflowers of Evil

I was in the Luau Lounge pondering my unpublished destiny when Charles Baudelaire took the stool next to me. "Call me Chuck," he said, grabbing a fistful of *fromage* goldfish crackers.

We talked about romance and poetry, about inspiration and talent and why the Cubs had not won the World Series since 1908.

"Absinthe!" he cried.

"Absinthe makes the heart grow fonder," I said.

The bartender's face needed a nap. "That green swill from Europe? It's illegal."

"Pernod then, *espèce de con!*"

She emptied Chuck's choked ashtray. "Your lungs must look like fresh asphalt."

Baudelaire gazed at his lap. "My lungs were not the organ that betrayed me."

I steered him away from spirochetes and tincture of mercury. "*The Flowers of Evil*, Chuck. Hell of a book."

The poet tapped his temple. "Forget Valentine's Day just once, *mon vieux*, and you'll find out what I meant."

Commotion erupted at the coconut-shell door. The Samoan bouncer held aloft a scowling adolescent in knickers and a beret. Baudelaire guffawed as the kid kicked and squirmed.

"It's that little punk Artie Rimbaud, getting carded!"

"I am the great Rimbaud!"

"If you're Rambo," the Samoan sneered, "I'm Robert Redford."

"I wrote 'The Drunken Boat'!"

"What happens on cruise ships ain't my business. The Luau don't serve minors since the last time they shut us down."

The poet's heaving chest was crisscrossed with bandoliers. "Nobody disses Rimbaud!"

"Yeah, not even the whole Vietnamese army. Now blow."

Rimbaud's eyes lit up, until he realized that meant he was supposed to leave. He flashed a double-barrel bird in our direction.

"You're overrated, Baudelaire! *Reader's Digest* wants your reeking poems!"

Chuck sniffed as if last week's *poisson* had been left under the radiator. "Damn Verlaine for not having better aim when he shot him." Baudelaire oozed negative capability, with a *soupçon* of stoicism for flavor.

The bouncer flung the kid out. Rimbaud's adenoidal whine pierced through a side window.

"Cubs suck, Bawdy Lair! Your poems should be in public toilets, then they'd finally be good for something!"

"He's *vert* with envy because I got another NEA grant," Chuck confided—as if I didn't know already from my umpteenth rejection letter from the same source.

"Yo, Body Hair! I just scored a MacArthur! Sixty grand a year till I'm old enough to vote, and I don't even have to fart for it!"

"C'est de la politique!" Chuck spat. "Who does that *petit* worm know on the committee?"

Heated moans blared from the bowels of the Bridges of Madison County pinball game. A figure wearing wooden shoes and earmuffs hunched over the box, masterfully fingering the buttons. Hardly anyone played that machine now, though at one time citizens had inexplicably lined up to feed it vast sums of money, despite the fact that it only gave you two balls. They were enormous balls, though, and constructed of the shiniest brass ever seen.

The pinball warlock furiously racked up points.

"Forty fucking million!" he crowed. "A record! I am an artiste!"

Chuck grimaced poetically. "*Mon dieu*, van Gogh, get a grip. It's only a damn game." Then, in a *sotto* voce titter: "Friends, Romans, countrymen, lend me your ear."

Vincent pointed a finger down his throat. "Golly, Evil Flower, that's real original."

"Like painting a vase of sunflowers is so cutting edge. Pull your thumb out of the dike and smell the coffee."

"Nice mixed metaphor. You might have a future writing Hallmark cards."

"Yeah, with lame pictures of sunflowers on them. Or skies full of whirlpools like somebody's flushing them down the crapper."

"Spoken like a true bourgeois." Van Gogh gazed starry-eyed at his tally on the machine, the angular four followed by seven plump, insatiable zeroes. "I'm flying to Tokyo tomorrow to do the sets for the new Godzilla film. I have a yen for the serious simoleons those exotic Orientals throw around."

"The lucky *cochon*," Baudelaire whimpered. "Godzilla is almost as brilliant as Jerry Lewis. Is there no end to a poet's pain?"

At least you got the NEA grant, I thought. I have to make due with enough rejection slips to wallpaper the Moulin Rouge.

Chuck drained his drink. "Man will not merely endure," he said with tears in his eyes, "he will prevail." He stumbled out without looking back, leaving nary a centime.

The bartender slapped the check in front of me.

"What does it matter?" I muttered into my cup. "In a century we'll all be dead and no one will be reading us anyway."

Robert Scotellaro

Bookends

I'd just jotted down an idea for a poem when the two pit bulls bolted from the bushes. One positioned its snout against my rear and the other deep into my groin. They looked like small sharks with feet. I stopped, forgetting how to breathe.

I was in a park I'd often driven past but had never been to before. It seemed a good place for a walk.

"Who you with?" a voice said.

When I turned to look, the dogs dug in deeper, snarling.

"Don't move, asshole, less you wanna go from a *he* to a *she*."

"Whoa . . ."

"I'll ask you again—who you with?"

"Just me," I said.

"You a wise-ass?"

"Sorry," I said, without knowing what I was apologizing for. He stepped in front of me, a full head shorter with a nasty twist to his mouth, his head tilted to one side. He wore a red hoodie and pointed to my chest. His dogs seemed content enough bookending the slim volume I'd become.

"Your colors," he said, "you're sporting your colors."

"This?" I followed his eyes, pointed to the top of my running suit.

"Don't play with me, man."

Confusion merged with panic. It was an awful mix. "This shirt?" I asked, tugging at the material.

"Them's CLD colors," he said. "Don't play dumb, sucka'."

"You mean like a gang? I'm not in a gang. I'm a poet."

"Faggot," he said.

My running suit was getting saliva-basted and I simultaneously anticipated unbearable pain and sudden loss.

"You don't wear blue in this park," he said. He did some kind of hand gestures, curling his wrists and forming his fingers into a distinct pattern and shot them in front of my face.

"But it's not blue," I told him.

"That's blue," he insisted.

"Actually it's kind of green. But I can see how it might look blue in this light."

He had a thin V-shaped goatee that he scratched with one finger.

I was hoping his dogs wouldn't attempt anything impromptu. He reached in his back pocket, removed a narrow paint chip book and fanned it out. "You gonna be missing some parts if you bullshitting me."

"Green," I repeated in a little voice.

He held a panel of graduated hues against my running top. I peered down.

"See?" I said. "Sassy Grass. Well, sort of between Sassy Grass and Kryptonite Green."

"Hmmm," he said, tilting the sample against my chest. "You just mighta hit the jackpot, sucka'." He twisted his fingers up into that configuration again, which seemed to mean so much to him, flashing it in front of my eyes. Then he said something in a foreign language or a slang I couldn't understand, and the pit bulls relented—flanked him as he walked back through the bushes.

I stood there for a moment with the sun on me, as though I were defrosting, with the word *Kryptonite* knocking around in my head, thinking: Go figure, some fake element from an imagined world just saved my ass.

SHELLIE ZACHARIA

What to Do on a Saturday Night One Week After Your Lover Announced, "Sayonara, Sweetheart," Even Though He's Not Japanese and He Never Called You Sweetheart Before

Go to the bookstore and read books you won't buy. Try not to bend or curl the paperback covers. Sit in a wingback chair and stare at all the people who go to a bookstore at night. See how the man in a wingback chair not far from you is curling the paperback cover of a fantasy novel. Hope he will buy the book and not just put it back on the shelf. Assume from his slouched posture and easy smile that he is delighted by warlocks and wizards and space travel. Remember that you are not. Be happy for this reader when a woman comes up behind him and taps her ringed hand on his head. Watch the two walk off. Sigh when you see he's left the book on the chair. Notice how some people look around nervously before they pick up something from erotica or self-help. Notice the two sections are next to each other and assume that erotic self-help is the answer. Hope that you don't see anyone engage in erotic self-help in the bookstore. Consider checking out these sections before you leave.

Strum on your guitar. In your dimly lit living room. Not in the bookstore. Decide to learn a new song and pull out your old songbook. First draw squiggly lines and smiley faces in the dust on the cover. Then pick a song at random. Try to play the guitar behind your head. Acknowledge it isn't easy. Sing and croon and howl. Stand by the window and let your voice warble and flutter. Sing with other people in mind. Sing like Johnny Cash. Frank Sinatra. Aretha Franklin. End with a Janis Joplin voice. People will hear you, even if you think they can't. Swish your hair around and throw yourself upon couch pillows. Realize some neighbor thinks there's funny business going on in your apartment. Be happy you've given someone something to talk about.

Move to the bedroom. Make a puppet with an old red sock. Sew button eyes. Two different buttons: one big black eye, one tiny pearly one. Draw the nose with a Sharpie. Make it a triangle nose like a jack-o-lantern and remember when Halloween was the greatest, when you dressed up as a princess, a hobo, a vampire, a gypsy. Go to the hall closet and find the black lace shawl your grandmother sent you from Greece. Wrap it around your shoulders and finish your puppet. Yarn hair. Yellow. Avoid a blunt bob and cut the hair in jagged lines. Have the puppet talk like Madeline Kahn. Don't let it talk to you though. That would be crazy. Only allow it to talk to the air, the ceiling fan, the skylights, the moon as you walk by the window.

Mark Budman

On Demand

The novelist—call him Dick, because he is big and albino and has a crooked jaw like the whale in Herman Melville's novel—sits next to a woman, the protagonist of this story. Dick is trying to peek down her tight white top. They are alone on a bench in the church hall. She sells cookbooks to support her kid's music school, and she has offered to sell his novel as well.

"My publisher is Love Universe," he tells her. "Print on demand."

She nods. She has never met a novelist before. When she looks at him, butterflies flutter in her tummy. Unless they aren't butterflies, but bugs that crawl inside you when you sleep naked, and never leave. Does this mean she is in lust? It can't be sexual; she loves only her husband.

"There is no demand," Dick adds under his breath.

His elbow touches hers. The protagonist moves away. The man looks just a few years younger than her, so she is certain she's not a cougar. That thought reassures her. She has never had sex with a real writer. Her husband is a bookkeeper, and he prefers spreadsheets to spread legs and rumpled sheets.

She tells the novelist about her ten-year-old son. "You know, he got this big piano award at school last year. Do you have kids?"

He leans toward her. "You have skin like a peach. So smooth."

Corny, she thinks. I have to drive him away, but I must sound both gentle and smart. He is an intellectual, after all.

"You know," she says, looking away and wrinkling the skin of her forehead. "The Y chromosome is defective. Next to the X, it looks like it has a broken leg. Ergo, men are lame next to women."

She is very proud of her "ergo" and her metaphor. It's a bit confusing, even to her, but still...

"Love is not lame," he says.

She shifts in her chair. Her bottom in tight pants gets hot from the plastic. "What is your book about?"

She doesn't want to call him Dick anymore. She'd rather call him Ishmael. She has been published once herself, in *Smashed Potatoes Quarterly*.

"An aunt who has steamy sex with her nephew."

The protagonist blushes. She should have asked this question before she had offered to sell his book here. The hotness spreads from her bottom to her lower belly. She is sweating down there, too. Does it mean she is easy?

"Is that so?" she asks.

"There is a motel across the road," Dick/Ishmael whispers in her ear. "I'll pay the bill, naturally."

She gets up and glares at him, her ears on fire. "What do you think I am?"

He gets up, too. "You say no because I'm an albino? I bet you'd refuse sex with an African-American. Or with a Buddhist monk."

Two hours later—after she drove the kid home and made a feeble excuse to leave her husband for a bit—Ishmael raises his head from between her legs and grins.

She refused the motel, and insisted on a Holiday Inn. She paid the bill. He was a first time novelist and she thought he must be poor. She gave her name as Anaïs Nin, and had a hard time explaining to the clerk how to spell it.

She fights the urge to wrap her legs around his neck and strangle him. She can't do this. Not in this universe. Instead, she grins back and moans. The sound rises to the ceiling and beyond, perhaps trying to escape to the universe where love is more than an adjective in the publisher's name.

Ring Lardner

from The Young Immigrunts

Chapter 9
The Bureau of Manhattan

Isn't it about time said my mother as we past Spuyten Duyvil and entered the Bureau of Manhattan that we made our plans.

What plans said my father all my plans is all ready made.

Well then you might make me your confident suggested my mother with a quaint smirk.

Well then heres the dope uttered my father in a vage tone I am going to drop you at the 125 st station where you will only half to wait 2 hours and a 1/2 for the rest of the family as the train from the west is do at 350 at 125 st in the meen wile I will drive out to Grenitch with Bill and see if the house is ready and etc and if the other peaples train is on time you can catch the 4 4 and I an Bill will meet you at the Grenitch station.

If you have time get a qt of milk for David said my mother with a pail look.

What kind of milk arsked my dad.

Oh sour milk my mother screened.

As she was now in a pretty bad temper we will leave her to cool off for 2 hours and a 1/2 in the 125 st station and end this chapter.

Chapter 10
N.Y. to Grenitch 500.0

The lease said about my and my fathers trip from the Bureau of Manhattan to our new home the soonest mended. In some way ether I or he got balled up on the grand concorpse and next thing you know we was thretning to swoop down on Pittsfield.

Are you lost daddy I arsked tenderly.

Shut up he explained.

At lenth we doubled on our tracks and done much better as we finley hit New Rochelle and puled up along side a policeman with falling archs.

What road do I take for Grenitch Conn quired my father with poping eyes.

Take the Boston post replid the policeman.

I have all ready subscribed to one out of town paper said my father and steped on the gas so we will leave the flat foot gaping after us like a prune fed calf and end this chapter.

Chapter 11
How It Ended

True to our promise we were at the station in Grenitch when the costly train puled in from 125 st. Myself and father hoped out of the lordly moter and helped the bulk of the family off of the train and I aloud our nurse and my 3 brothers to kiss me tho Davids left me rarther moist.

Did you have a hard trip my father arsked to our nurse shyly.

Why no she replid with a slite stager.

She did too said my mother they all acted like little devils.

Did you get Davids milk she said turning on my father.

Why no does he like milk my father replid with a gastly smirk.

We got lost mudder I said brokenly.

We did not screened my father and accidently cracked me in the shins with a stray foot.

To change the subjeck I turned my tensions on my brother Jimmie who is nerest my age.

I've seen our house Jimmie I said brokenly I got here first.

Yes but I slept all night on a train and you didn't replid Jimmie with a dirty look.

Nether did you said my brother John to Jimmie you was awake all night.

Were awake said my mother.

Me and david was awake all night and crid said my brother John.

But I only crid once the whole time said my brother Jimmie.

But I didn't cry at all did I I arsked to my mother.

So she replid with a loud cough Bill was a very very good boy.

So now we will say fare well to the characters in this book.

GAIL WRONSKY

DEATH OF THE AUTHORS

Nighttime in the City of Angels. Artificial daylight shines on a closed-off section of Lincoln Boulevard; a black 1940s sedan hunches by with an iconic blonde inside; movie industry cops loiter lumpishly around a taco truck. Four stories above, in a faculty office devoid of books except for the CliffsNotes of Machiavelli's *The Prince*, a man in a cashmere V-neck comes to the end of another auto-erotic asphyxiation, catches his breath, changes his trousers, sits behind his gigantic computer screen and types.

Dear English Department:

While the recent loss of our creative writing faculty has been a hard pill for all of us to swallow, so to speak, I want to say that as your Chair I've been profoundly moved by your discretion. I believe, now more than ever, and as we agreed, it's best that we not discuss the matter here on University grounds. After all, our students pay a great deal of money precisely so that they won't be bothered by depressing things. Thus I've decided (I'm sure you'll all support me on this) not to disrupt our annual student-faculty soiree with any kind of memorial tribute for those we've lost. I sincerely believe that Ron and Edie, who always had the best interests of our students at heart, would have agreed.

I'd like to take this opportunity to congratulate Carl, our new Director of Writing: Let's Talk About Me. (The former Creative Writing Program was renamed, you'll remember, in response to the Dean's call for greater truth-in-advertising). Carl, having never taken a writing workshop, will be bringing new ideas to the table, and, having never published a story or poem, will not be unduly influencing our impressionable young writers with his personal style.

One small, if discouraging, announcement: sometime during the next month or two you will each be interviewed by LAPD's homicide division. It's merely a formality, I assure you; none of us are "people of interest," but I want to make certain we present a unified (how could we not?) front. The facts, as you surely remember them, are as such: during a department meeting last April, three crucial votes were taken. The first concerned furniture arrangement in the lounge; the second, "Anon." vs. "Anonymous—are they really one and the same?; the third, whether or not we should, as a department, issue a statement reflecting our belief in the death of literature. Only two ballots kept us, each time, from reaching what should have been a seamless consensus. Though the voting was private, we all knew that the holdouts were Ron and Edie, may they rest in peace. Later that day, our two writers went to the zoo—no doubt in order to amble and reflect, to reconsider their adversarial position in regards to departmental agendas. Horrible as it now is to recall, two masked criminals who have yet to be apprehended approached them from behind and, totally at random it appears, shoved them both over a cement barrier and into the lion habitat, where they were devoured immediately. We found out the following day and grieved as one.

If I have misrepresented any of this, please correct me. As for alibis, heaven forbid we should need them, please remember that the entire department, with the exceptions of myself and Carl, attended Marianne's baby shower in Playa Vista that afternoon. Carl and I, you probably recall without my having to remind you, were on our way to Mexico in order to deliver clothing to Almas Perdidas, the orphanage I've visited and supported, with the help of Campus Ministry, for many years. The orphans themselves, if I understood their Spanish correctly (or they my Spanish!) have offered to verify our whereabouts if that were to become necessary, which is unthinkable.

So much for unpleasantness. I promise that once these police interrogations are over we'll put all this friction behind us, moving forward toward a future of smiling collegiality and even more enthusiastic, if that's possible, agreement. Last week's unanimous vote in favor of diversity was indicative of what's ahead.

Peace, blessings, and zero tolerance for intolerance,
Your Chair

On the street below, spotlights go out. Celebrities ooze into limos and head off into glittery, booze-soaked nights of club hopping and famousness. Traffic returns. The department chair, looking both ashamed and resentful, like a grown child whose mother still dresses him—no, looking pasty and evil, like an anthrax-laced quesadilla—clicks "send," and logs back on to the David Carradine fansite.

Paul Blaney

Later at Cana

But then of course there had to be one: an ingrate, curmudgeon, a complainer in spite of all. Remarking sotto voce that it was all very wonderful, but why not a more complex vintage then? Why not something with a bit of body? And of course He had to go and catch the comment—always did have sharp ears—and of course He didn't take it kindly. Not a word, but you should have seen the look. A look that said, I see you; I never forget a face. Just the sort of look you *don't* want from someone like Him. I felt rather sorry for the old grouch. There won't be any wine to critique where he's going.

Sean Lovelace

I Love Bocce

There was a time I thought most everyone should play bocce. I was like Rico Daniele, author of *Bocce: A Sport For Everyone* and president of the Wonderful World of Bocce Association, who would say to anyone, "Let's get bocce courts in school and playgrounds for the kids, parents, and grandparents."

I wasn't well.

I was in nursing school and that was plenty. I had an unrequited crush on a girl named Paige. I had a chronically sore Achilles tendon and couldn't exercise.

Overall, I was slightly depressed.

This is what the university therapist said:

"You're confusing your feelings for a young lady with the game she introduced you to. It's classic transference."

"You have to let it go."

"I'm not one of those New York shrinks with a fancy office."

"Everything isn't about bocce."

Of course, everything wasn't about bocce. But tell that to my world.

Example, the very next day:

My OR rotation and we were standing around a blue-mummied patient with a defunct gallbladder. There was the head surgeon and me and my nursing instructor and a medical student and a circulating nurse with long, stringy hair—like something out of a clogged drain, etc.—and a scrub nurse and a nurse anesthetist with a sad smile.

My instructor and I were only observing. We'd been going about an hour, routine stuff, clamp this, cut here, watch that bleeder, and so on, when the head surgeon yelled out, "Anyone here like bocce?"

I startled, and sweat popped up on my forehead.

"I dated an Italian guy who was crazy about it," the circulating nurse said, following the surgeon's lead. "Liked bocce so much he would shoot the balls out of a replica cannon, or store them in the refrigerator fruit drawer. Sometimes, he'd swallow the balls, and, well

. . . wait."

"That's what I mean," the surgeon said, as he sutured a neat bow over a vein. "Dedication. Extractor."

Handing over the extractor, the scrub nurse added, "I once played a round with inflatable bocce balls, inflated with helium, at a side-show in Indiana."

"I like bocce as well as anyone," the medical student said. He followed the surgeon's fingers as they lifted a lung. "I once drove a convertible bocce ball cross country."

Everyone ignored the student. He was trying to impress the surgeon.

The nurse anesthetist sighed and said, "The last man off a bocce court rarely looks back."

We all nodded our heads. I felt like a cloud in someone else's dream.

"Has anyone seen a snake that's eaten a bocce ball?" said the surgeon. "Suction." He stood away as the scrub nurse cleared the surgical field. "I did once. In Africa. I was up 13-4 on a group of native chaps—Masabis or what not—and a cobra snatched my ball, of course couldn't digest it." He paused and snipped away a layer of fascia. No one answered him. Surgeons were always assuming everyone routinely traveled to Africa.

"I played in Haiti," the medical student said, "with coconuts, during a tournament. I actually grouped the balls so close that several laws of physics were altered."

No answer. The Pulsox beeped; someone paged someone over the intercom.

Finally, the nurse anesthetist offered, "I play decent bocce when dreaming, or just unconscious. Compared to unconscious, my conscious bocce is nothing."

The surgeon grunted. "Now," he said, "I'm sure you're conscious bocce is something, too."

"Not at all," the nurse anesthetist said, reaching up to adjust the drip on an IV.

All this talk about bocce, I felt I was going to faint. I felt normal.

"I love bocce," I blurted out, and everyone turned to stare at me.

The surgeon frowned, eyed my instructor, and said, "Let's close this up."

Later, my instructor wrote me up for unprofessional behavior. To top it off she passed me a tiny bottle of Scope and said my breath smelled like pizza. I think it was pizza, but she may have said ravioli.

Genna Walker

On Collecting Porcelain Wiener Dogs

Collecting porcelain dogs is easy; you look left and buy a cute little poodle, look right and buy a robust, regal Dane. The real challenge, as any real collector knows, is in wiener dogs. Does not the very thought of it set your toes to tingling? The rush of blood is hard to handle, but the thrill of a good score is the greatest feeling one may ever experience.

Some collectors think that they can handle the challenge of acquiring these porcelain puppies before they are truly ready, a mistake that causes professionals to wince and turn away from embarrassment. It takes a certain skill set to acquire such a prize.

Of course, there are always a few lucky ones who stumble upon a real find: matching salt and pepper shakers of adorably cute wiener dogs, matching collars painted around their necks. The real professionals eventually hunt them down, put them in their scopes, and take the kill. A simple transaction completed, and suddenly Aunt Sally is showing off her nice new pair.

Pride in a collection is the hallmark of the profession. This isn't any silly hobby; much is put at stake in this overzealous market. Women everywhere, of course, are forever aware of how hard it is to find a worthwhile wiener dog. Everyone has heard what they say at all of the markets: all of the good ones are either broken or taken. There's a stiff competition out there searching for the same goods. The presence of large, misleading packages leads to many disappointed ladies.

These packages may seem to offer up the pleasure of a very special porcelain creation, but oftentimes deliver something less than desired. One may wish for a lovely little pup, only to find another set of plastic lemons.

As part of such a prestigious group of collectors, it is paramount to know that, while no official meetings of the minds exist, certain gatherings are only spoken of in hushed voices. Brought together by a mutual love of the porcelain wiener dog, collectors exhibit their finest animals. Long, skinny, short, and fat; the dogs come in all sizes.

Arguers of size focus on the girth of your pup, claiming that if it is less than a handful, it won't ever please anyone. The lamentations of those who can never please with their inadequate dog length drown together in a single cry of anguish. People opposed to this field of thought, however, affirm that it is not the volume of the dog's bark that matters, but how well it frightens villains.

Besides, they whisper to one another, some people prefer a wiener dog that can fit in the palm of their hand. Who really wants something so large that they have to use two hands to stroke it?

The whole of this shady business was not enough to deter the average homemaker from entering the ring--a person's mother is not easy to be seen as a master collector. However, there she was on market day, clutching tightly to her chest a white box reputed to contain high quality merchandise.

Furtively, she passed money to the vendor and looked around her before tucking the box deep into her purse. I remembered when I used to believe that she hid the whole world in the depths of that bag--now I had trouble thinking of what other wonders she may have been hiding inside that mysterious sack.

I followed her; she stopped at all of the best tables. It seems my skills in collecting had not come from my own cultivation, but rather had been passed down genetically like my red hair and freckles. I lost track of her for a moment, then a hand firmly grasped my wrist. Turning, I looked into my mother's eyes, shocked that she found me following her.

"Hello, darling!"

"Mom! What are you doing here?" I asked, voice shaking.

"I took a detour this evening. Look at this cute little porcelain statue I bought!"

She reached inside her bag and displayed the box that I had imagined handling myself some day. Lips parted, she removed the lid and pulled out her prize wrapped in white tissue paper. Flashes of red were revealed slowly; a small rooster rested in her hands.

"Isn't it lovely?" she said. "Don't you just want to touch it?"

Joe Clifford

Fair Shake

Emily and Ashley Varner were older than Jimmy. He wasn't sure how much older exactly, but both had their license, so older than him. The lake house where Jimmy's family spent their summers sat next to the Varners' on the shores of North Tahoe. Being around Emily and Ashley for those two months was the highlight of his year, even if it meant having to bunk with his older stepbrother, Toby, who, aside from occasionally picking him up from soccer practice, was pretty much a useless dipshit.

Jimmy lay in the Varners' backyard, Ashley sunning herself on the wood deck above, Emily in the grass below, teasing him, as usual.

"You still a virgin, Jimmy?" Emily asked, poking his belly.

Jimmy wriggled.

"Leave him alone, Em."

Emily flopped on her stomach, grabbed his wrist. "You have any pot?"

Ashley peered over the railing.

"No," Jimmy said.

Ashley leaned back.

"I mean, not on me."

Jimmy had no idea where to get pot. He never smoked the stuff. There were guys at school he could ask, maybe. But at Tahoe?

It was a total desperation move asking Toby, who read *Harry Potter* books and spent most of his time playing *World of Warcraft* on his computer.

"Of *course*," Toby replied, pasty, pimply face peeping over the top of *Prisoner of Azkaban*. "Villa Roma. The Italian restaurant on South Lake. Crazy Mark."

"Crazy Mark?"

"He works in the kitchen. He's got brain damage. My friend

Kyle bought some of the pot off him. He's got the best shit."

"Problem is," Jimmy said. "I don't have any money."

"Me neither. But no worries," said Toby. "Check this out." Toby pulled a folder from beneath his printer, passing along a sheet of paper, which had rows of twenty-dollar bills.

They looked like shit, worse than Monopoly money, printed on regular Xerox paper, stiff as a baseball card.

You'd *have* to be brain damaged to think these were real.

Driving back from Villa Roma, Jimmy couldn't believe they'd pulled this off. He'd expected some longhair to come running out the restaurant with a shotgun. Police sirens. Something. But nothing.

There on Toby's lap sat the giant bag of weed.

"He just took . . . the money?"

"Didn't look twice."

"How'd you meet this guy again?"

"My friend, Kyle."

Jimmy had had never seen Toby with any friends, not back home, not here either. "Who's Kyle?"

"Another gamer I met online."

What did Jimmy care? Emily and Ashley Varner were waiting next door.

Walking beneath the tall pines into the backyard, Jimmy felt the thrill of being bad.

"I can't believe you got it!" Emily said.

"Had to go to the South Lake. That's where my guy is." Which Jimmy thought sounded pretty cool. "He has the best shit."

He passed the bag to Emily, who opened it and inhaled. Her face turned nasty. "Maybe if you were making pizza. It's fucking oregano, Jimmy."

"I told you he was just a kid," Ashley said.

How could he be so stupid as to count on Toby? This is why he never talked to the guy. Dumbass bought fake drugs with fake money. He'd made Jimmy look like a fool.

Toby sat at his computer, headset on like he thought he was a real goddamn pilot, rapidly firing at make-believe monsters. Fucktard was going to graduate next year, and he lived in a fantasy world.

"How goes the dungeons and dragons?" Jimmy said with a sneer.

Toby flipped off his headset and spun around, hands behind his head, completely oblivious.

Jimmy wanted to punch him in his stupid pimply face. He looked around Toby's side of the room. Lord Voldemort posters above the bed, Proactive bottles strewn about the floor. And he was stuck with this goofy bastard for a brother the rest of his life.

"Thanks for today," Toby said. "I don't get to do that stuff often."

"Do what? Score weed?"

"No, hang out with friends. It was fun. We should do it again sometime."

Through the open windows, Jimmy heard the girls climb into their convertible, giggling loudly. The Tahoe sun was low, casting the room a burnt orange.

Jimmy turned back downstairs.

"Hey, Jimmy," Toby called out. "I forgot to ask. How'd your girlfriends like the pot?"

The girls revved the engine next door and cranked the radio, tires spinning down the long mountain road, their laughter carrying into the distance.

"Best shit they ever had," Jimmy shouted over his shoulder.

Craig Fishbane

Poets at the Boarding House

Billy Collins used to visit me every morning. Those were the days when I lived on the top floor of a boarding house overlooking a small park with a playground. Before Billy started making regular appearances, I spent most of my time staring out the window, watching pigeons gather on lampposts. Seated on the edge of a saggy twin bed, I would observe avian mating rituals and battles over slices of stale bread. I sat with a keyboard perched on my lap, waiting for new poems to flock to my fingers. I had started to wonder if my true calling was not literature but ornithology.

Billy made a habit of arriving at dawn, often greeting me with fresh coffee and blueberry muffins. I can't say I ever enjoyed being roused from my dreams at sunrise, but something about the way he smiled under his wayward wisps of grey hair—and something about the smell of that Colombian brew—made me amenable to these daily visitations.

He usually tended to the room while I had breakfast, adjusting pictures on the wall and folding down the bedding. After I had finished eating, he would wipe the dust off the screen of my laptop to reveal a welcoming whiteness, a clear cool surface that invited me to ice skate across the screen. He would lead me in a liquid-crystal dance each morning on the frozen pond of my PC. When the final movement was completed, he would straighten his tie and excuse himself to tend to his garden.

I rarely had any more company until midnight. I took advantage of those empty hours to catch up on both my reading and my sleep. I had to. When Charles Bukowski showed up—as he did on most evenings—there was never any time to either rest or reflect. He would slam the door open, screaming to startle me out of bed. Then he'd toss me a can from a six-pack. We would drink for hours, swapping stories and dirty jokes. Some nights we visited the whores across the hall. Later we'd return to my room and trash the wallpaper and bed sheets. Even my laptop got tossed out the window once or twice.

When I was with Bukowski, I didn't need it. Everything I wrote was spray-painted on the walls: lyrics to songs you could only sing in a back alley. We would chant each chorus together, drinking from a bottle of Jack Daniels we had stolen from the hookers. When we ran out of liquor, Bukowski would give me a playful punch on the shoulder and then head back to his own flophouse to sleep off the next day's hangover.

I thought that things could go on like this forever until one night Bukowski stayed too late. I had gotten a bottle of Wild Turkey for my birthday and he didn't want to leave until we had finished it. The sun was coming up by the time he stumbled to the door and, after a few tries, opened it. Billy Collins was waiting on the other side, holding a paper bag that smelled of croissants and freshly-brewed espresso.

I don't think either one of them knew what to do. Billy Collins forced himself to smile as Bukowski scratched his ass. He offered a pensive sigh when Bukowski farted. They continued to stand at the threshold, the outlaw and the laureate, sizing each other up, frozen in an unspoken impasse. I was afraid they might never move until each man flinched at the sound of agitated footsteps approaching from the hallway. Emily Dickinson was shaking her head as she adjusted the bun in her hair.

She wanted to know when I was going to pay the rent.

Meg Tuite

Catwoman Unplugged

I heard over and over how glamorous and rocking Catwoman was, but I was the one who clipped her nose hair and whiskers from her chin before anyone got a look at her. I bound her in her girdle first and then her rubber suit. Believe me, it was no easy task. Her flesh was loaded, packed with days away from the gym, macking on McDonald's drive-thru. I zipped her in with extreme caution, sitting on her like she was a suitcase I was trying to close. Zipper teeth had bitten her more than a few times and she had scars to prove it. She kept her fingernails long and jagged to scratch me. I had the scars to prove it.

How much Botox can a post-menopausal superhero endure? Time doesn't care if you used to climb the sides of buildings, whip arch enemies or shoot darts at them. Batman wore hair plugs and took Viagra when he needed to lift off, and things that used to ignite on their own needed a little nudge. There was some beauty in growing older. Batman and Robin finally came out of the closet, got married. It was a quiet wedding. The Joker was their best man.

Catwoman had her moments when she was called to action. It used to be a lift-off straight from cement to villain, but now we took the elevator to at least the third floor before I sent her bloated body into space.

Most of her gigs were in malls now. Kids waited in line to get an autograph and a photo of her sneering and hissing at the camera. I won't even go into how many liposuction appointments she had. She was the bomb. I had always lusted for her, though there was no pretense she was the hot Catwoman every one believed existed when I situated her spandex so airtight that no fat leakage was visible, and her schedule so she always had another event to keep the money dribbling in. She was poor and lumpy, but so was I.

One night she snagged a sleazebag before he grabbed an old lady's purse. The lady thrashed him unconscious while Catwoman held him down. Catwoman always enjoyed audience participation.

She blasted in on some lowlifes about to initiate the virgin arm of a girl into heroin and her less virgin reproductive zone into gang rape. Catwoman powed and kazoomed the scumbags, then flattened the girl against her, hauled her back to her house intact. "Keep your panties in place and your brothers in space," she said, before hoisting herself up onto a brick wall. She always loved a good rhyme, visualized a rocket before fluttering off in a butterfly haze into the shadows.

How do you tell a superhero that you love her? I washed her delicates by hand for decades. I sent her favorite chocolates anonymously. She assumed they were from The Green Hornet as she stuffed them in her mouth lying on the bed watching episodes of "The Bachelor." He'd been after her ass since 1999. I'd been after her ass since 1986.

So we're in this hotel room in Rapid City, Iowa. Not a lot of action for Catwoman, except for the college campuses; date rape and all. It was a slow night. I was sweating and shaking like some kind of vestal virgin as I came out of the bathroom wearing a towel. I was tongue-swollen by all the years of misuse, lack. I stood there while Catwoman sucked in Cheetos and flipped channels lying on her bed. Of course, it was always a room with two doubles.

"What?" she asked.

"What? I asked.

"Hey, I was just thinking." She crammed a fistful of Cheetos in her mouth. "Get me a gig on 'Chelsea Lately.' She's getting big and I could snag some serious coverage with her. Plus I think she digs the tough chicks."

I had a bewildered look on my face when I dropped my towel. I smelled of hotel products. My hair was uncombed, rabid. My body displayed all its dimples, cellulite and strange corners. I inhaled deeply and threw myself on top of her. It was a leaping lunge. More than she had been capable of in a long while.

She stared up at me while I dripped down on her, looking into those hollow, hound dog eyes that were usually hidden beneath a mask.

"What?" she asked.

I clamped down on those shriveled lips and bit them. Her eyes were wide, bloodshot as a sunset.

"Listen, bitch," I said. "Who's the superhero now?"

She didn't say another word all night.

Steve Almond

Unfriendly Cashiers

Not rude, which would imply all the tired grudges against fate (as would bitter or hard-bitten) or impervious, with its slender caprice. Just unfriendly, as in: not interested in being your friend. Not interested in your clothing, or chummy witticisms, or what you're buying today, just there at the register with a nametag.

My favorites work at down-in-the-mouth markets, the leaky emporiums with carts that are a tetanus threat and off brands whose lettering croons sweetly off-key. What I like second-best about them is that they watch everything, a step ahead of your complaints and stupid coupons, tired of your voice before you even speak. These are men and women immune to mood, generous only in competence. You and your strawberry soda and salsa and your low-watt public friendliness face? *They don't care.*

Make a joke and they'll stare at you like you're naked and disappointing.

What I like best about them is this stout refusal to prettify the situation, to obey the cursed slogans of our age, with its pathological ulteriority and salesmanship, with its spirit the color and composition of hotdogs.

And best of all: those moments when something unusual and true and funny happens, when a spoiled kid throws up from too many animal crackers or the unctuous new bag boy rams a plate-glass window or the manager slips on the ice outside, on her ass, and the cashiers, all in a row and against every grain of better judgment, grin.

Joe Mills

Toy Story

Having been sent to get a birthday present, one under twenty dollars, he loops the unfamiliar aisles more and more slowly until finally he just grinds to a stop in front of a shelf of Barbies dressed like doctors. Her exact specialty isn't clear. She's probably something like a radiologist or ophthalmologist, so she doesn't actually have to put her hands in the messy parts of the body. Plus there's no need for a Proctologist Barbie or urologist or gynecologist, when any potential patient just has a slick plastic curve for a crotch. He scans the shelves and realizes Dr. Barbie comes after Princess Barbie, Rockstar Barbie, and Chef Barbie, but before Racecar Driver Barbie, Lifeguard Barbie, and Computer Software Engineer Barbie. Each one has a job. A good one. No Bartender Barbie. Waitress Barbie. Hotel Housekeeper Barbie. No Recently Fired Barbie.

How does she do it? How does she get these jobs? What credentials does she have? By now her résumé must be ten pages long. She gets hired again and again. Without re-training. Without ever having a counselor spending a mandatory fifteen minutes with her, explaining unemployment benefits, and suggesting this might be an opportunity to think outside the box. Only her breasts have ever been downsized. Maybe the unemployment rate is so high because Barbie has all the fucking jobs. It's not fair, and something needs to be done about it. Just once she needs to be the one terminated, so he reaches for the gun he's been carrying around lately, ever since his own meeting, because that's how a story like his goes, and he knows once he takes it out there are only a couple of endings. He'll fire at Barbie after Barbie until the bullets run out, and he'll become a joke on Leno and Letterman—the fat middle-aged laid-off executive responsible for the Barbie Massacre—or he'll turn the gun on himself.

Except the pocket is empty.

He begins mechanically patting the other ones as if searching for his keys, and he keeps doing it even after he realizes his wife must have stripped him of it as he left, tidying him with the same deft skill she uses to wipe their children's faces as they go out the door.

By the time a salesperson comes along and asks, "Can I help you?" he has wound down to the point that he only can make spasmodic half-gestures towards the towering wall of perky breasts and corporate smiles. "Barbie," he gasps. "Barbie. Boxed in."

"Of course," the woman says, sliding a white-coated doll from the shelf. "I'll take it up front for you, and just let me know if I can help with anything else."

Marisela Navarro

The Defenestration of Prince Eric

Max, dressed up as Mr. Rogers in a red cardigan, black tie, brown dress pants, and sideways-slicked hair, was standing in some bedroom breeze, his right hand stuffed inside a King Friday XIII puppet, left hand uncharted, shaking in his loafers after having thrown Eric, best friend and best dressed, out the first floor window.

Penny stood in the doorway open-mouthed, body-painted in such a way as to make it look like she wasn't naked, but she clearly was naked, and this may have been what started all the trouble. Her breasts were green with tones of gray, exactly the color of Frankenstein, except she was going as Nature. To complicate her look further, she exhaled large puffs of cigarette smoke regularly and mindlessly, so someone guessed her to be a foggy swamp.

The defenestration was unplanned. Max was not particularly a strong type so he was somewhat startled with himself, uncertain how he'd managed to pick up his friend and hurl him through the screen. He imagined his left hand had grabbed Eric's collar and King Friday XIII had grabbed the back of Eric's tights with his whole puppet head, and that somehow, he'd scooped him up like a hawk would a field mouse. This was a little far-fetched considering Max was often mistaken for being a Leesburg High Yellow Jacket, even though he was, in fact, a UCF Knight, but then again, unbelievable feats of strength can happen in pent-up men, and years ago on a baseball field, a big kid had rubbed a baseball in the dirt and ordered Max to lick it or get his head beaten into oatmeal vomit. Max chose "lick it." It was the safest, although more disgusting, of the two options.

The decision to lick had seemed like an isolated incident; but though Eric had screen tangled in his hair and landscaping abrasions, in need of a comb and a pair of clean tights, and despite the fact that Max had loved Penny all his life and dreamed of one day building her a castle, all he wanted now was to lick Nature off her body.

Penny's costume was complete with a blackberry bush that rustled around her hips as she walked. The blackberries were real (she'd been saying so the whole night), and all night long, Max had been eating them in his mind, looking pretty triumphant with the fact that he'd won the competition, the one in his mind where the guys moshed for Penny's berries in a party pit. He was, after all, the trustworthy one, the obvious hunter-gatherer.

Two minutes before the incident, Max and Eric had been in the bedroom talking about the greatest movie scenes ever, away from the party chaos, beats thumping the floor beneath them. Then Eric nonchalantly said, "I'd love to bang Penny's melons." He knew Max was crazy for her, but somehow, the fact that she was naked at the party made it seem like an okay thing to say, like a free pass.

Penny's melons made Max uncomfortable for many reasons, but mostly it was this un-Mr. Rogers-like arousal he was experiencing in front of her, and something else too—though he didn't want to admit it, he was jealous of Penny, because she had advanced to the next level with her uninhibited freedom and lack of concern for the judgment of others, a state of being he could never achieve, but if he could, right now, at this party, achieve an equivalent version of it, he'd be walking around with a swinging, painted ball sack, and did he really want to do that? No, he didn't want to, which meant he could never have Penny because she'd never love a guy who didn't go balls out, figuratively and literally. He was dressed as Mr. Rogers after all, no one at this party even knowing who Mr. Rogers was, they just thought he was wearing a cardigan for the hell of it, and here was Eric, dressed up as the handsome Prince Eric from *The Little Mermaid*, in blue tights, satin red sash, and a white seamless V-neck dress shirt, basically the equivalent of going balls out while fully dressed. So when Penny opened the door and blew a cloud of swampy fog in their direction and sang in her best Ariel impersonation, "Watch and you'll see, someday I'll be, part of your world," chucking Eric headfirst, disgusting as it was, seemed like the safest option.

Sean Thomas

A One-Night Stand With Art

I was playing keyboards in a post-punk-indie-rock band and working in a factory that assembled motorized wheelchairs when I met her. She'd been sent over from the temp agency for an eight-hour day at the factory, but at lunchtime she bit into a Mr. Goodbar and told me that minimum wage was a scam and she was going to drink whiskey at the bar down the street. She said her name was Art, and asked if I wanted to come with her. Liking the sound of that double-entendre, and post-punk-indie-rock star that I was, I agreed.

We sat at the bar and drank Wild Turkey. We chain smoked Gauloises and crossed and re-crossed our legs. We puffed a joint behind the dumpster in the parking lot. Then we walked back inside and made out in the men's bathroom, on the toilet and the sink and the floor, where she told me between kisses that work was meaningless and I should quit my job, forever, because other things were far more important, like literature and painting and sculpting and photography and video and dance and music. Like Art, she said.

Later, after we stumbled into her apartment, I gazed at the preschool-style finger paintings on her walls and decided she was right. I told her I would never work again, and I would dedicate myself to Art, to post-punk-indie-rock in particular. She said it was a good idea, as long as I didn't mean her when I said Art, and we tore off our clothes.

We were drunk and stoned, and I lost myself in her skin. We tangled on the couch and I kissed the contours of her hips and inner thighs. I shut my eyes, and in my head I pictured piano keys, chipped and dusted, violas and violins, drums and cymbals, and a muted trumpet blaring needles of red and yellow haze.

"Max Ernst!" she cried as I pressed my tongue against her. "Franz Kline and Jackson Pollock died in the sunset!" She grabbed my ears and pulled my head up to her chest, and she told me that painters died every day for their paintings and writers wrote every day or died.

She said that Art mimicked life, made it a better place, taught us how to see ourselves, was completely patriarchal, and had ceased to exist five hundred years ago.

I told her she was crazy.

And she said it was best if I didn't talk, because in the end we were only masking our alienation, together, while the world spun out of control. Then she pushed my head back down between her legs and told me to kiss her again, and I had no choice, because after all, her name was Art.

Dan Wiencek

Thirteen Writing Prompts

1.
Write a scene showing a man and a woman arguing over the man's friendship with a former girlfriend. Do not mention the girlfriend, the man, the woman, or the argument.

2.
Write a short scene set at a lake, with trees and shit. Throw some birds in there, too.

3.
Choose your favorite historical figure and imagine if he/she had been led to greatness by the promptings of an invisible imp living behind his or her right ear. Write a story from the point of view of this creature. Where did it come from? What are its goals? Use research to make your story as accurate as possible.

4.
Write a story that ends with the following sentence: Debra brushed the sand from her blouse, took a last, wistful look at the now putrefying horse, and stepped into the hot-air balloon.

5.
A wasp called the tarantula hawk reproduces by paralyzing tarantulas and laying its eggs into their bodies. When the larvae hatch, they devour the still living spider from the inside out. Isn't that fucked up? Write a short story about how fucked up that is.

6.
Imagine if your favorite character from 19th-century fiction had been born without thumbs. Then write a short story about them winning the lottery.

7.
Write a story that begins with a man throwing handfuls of $100 bills from a speeding car, and ends with a young girl urinating into a tin bucket.

8.
A husband and wife are meeting in a restaurant to finalize the terms of their impending divorce. Write the scene from the point of view of a busboy snorting cocaine in the restroom.

9.
Think of the most important secret your best friend has ever entrusted you with. Write a story in which you reveal it to everyone. Write it again from the point of view of your friend. Does she want to kill you? How does she imagine doing it? Would she use a gun, or something crueler and more savage, like a baseball bat with nails in it?

10.
Popular music is often a good source of writing inspiration. Rewrite Bob Dylan's "Visions of Johanna" as a play.

11.
Write a short scene in which one character reduces another to uncontrollable sobs without touching him or speaking.

12.
Your main character finds a box of scorched human hair. Whose is it? How did it get there?

13.
A man has a terrifying dream in which he is being sawn in half. He wakes to find himself in the Indian Ocean, naked and clinging to a door; a hotel keycard is clenched in his teeth. Write what happens next.

Kelly Cherry

The Department of Mirth and Laughter

We are located in Paris, on the right side of the Left Bank. Where else? Where else is there so much bubbly, so much discreetly beautiful light that falls on roofs and the Seine, Notre Dame and sidewalk cafés?

To obtain your license for unlicensed behavior, you must apply in person. Please note: while the Department is generally inclined toward inclusivity, not everyone is welcome. Cynics, for example. We grant no permits to cynics. One more thing to be cognizant of: mirth and laughter are not the same thing. Mirth is an attitude; laughter is an activity.

Upon entering the building, look *à gauche*. You will see a door with an upper pane of frosted glass. The pane bears a pink tinge so you will enjoy a rosy view of it.

Knock. Maybe no one will answer. If so, that is because the staff is busy laughing. Knock again.

Someone will open, eventually. You will find yourself in a storeroom with racks of champagne, shelves of toys, displays of rollicking clowns. If a hand lifts your skirt just a tad, do not be offended too quickly: flirting is *de rigueur* here. But only flirting. Talk should not be too blue.

There are chocolates and candies, including lemon drops. There are pastries, especially croissants and sweet crêpes. Such tidy edibles are known to increase pleasure.

Immediately upon receipt of your license, handsome Frenchmen will kiss the back of your hand, tell you how gorgeous you are. They do this whether you are gorgeous or not. They do it because you have your license to licentious behavior. Also because they are Frenchmen. (Switch the sexes if you are male, if you want to switch them.)

In other rooms there are sofas and lounges, silk pillows, cool linen sheets. Everyone is laughing. Everyone is having a good time.

Do not expect card games, video games, or roulette. We find that our licensees become addicted to them, which takes all the fun out. For similar reasons, we allow no Internet access.

But the Department can make available yo-yos, Etch A Sketch tablets, watercolors, and rose petals to sprinkle on the cool linens. We also offer Slinkys and Shmoom (or Shmoos, if you prefer the other plural), as they are among the biggest laugh-getters.

We are always delighted how a light heart will lead to romance. And almost always it does.

Smoking is not allowed, not even by French philosophers.

There is no limit to how long you may stay. Time is limitless when one is having a good time.

Whenever you do choose to leave, we will present you with the small gift of a box of Merrimints. They are delicious, tingling, and life-affirming.

DovBer Naiditch

Interview with an Orthodox Jewish Vampire

Jews aren't supposed to be vampires. Not literal ones. That's for the *goyim*, like skiing and citrus flavored beers, so you could imagine my surprise. This is what you get for dating a *shiksa* I guess, though to be sure I thought otherwise when we started. Apparently not everyone who migrated over from the former Soviet Union to Pittsburgh did so for fear of religious persecution. But when you're partying at a club and a girl comes up to you and speaks with that kind of accent and doesn't have a giant silver cross hanging around her neck, you put two and two together. I just did the math wrong. And now I drink blood.

I know this sounds messed up, but I only drink Jewish blood. It doesn't make sense—it doesn't make it any more kosher or anything—but it's what I do. I drink a little bit here and there, from friends and family, though my *bubbe*, G-d bless her, always wants to feed me more. Take take, she says, take take. You know how Jewish grandmothers are. I don't have the heart to tell her it tastes bad, though. Too much garlic. It would kill her.

The light thing is the same. It messes up my prayer schedule because of my sleep patterns, and a lot of the *mitzvos*, too, are not meant for the nocturnal. But the rabbis at the *Yeshiva* I went to are really helpful. You wouldn't believe how much fun they had, even, with all of those rules and everything. Like can I even be part of a *Minyan*?

A *Minyan*? A quorum of ten men needed to pray. And here I'm a man, but not alive in the technical sense. The Nosferatu, the undead, you see. They had to go to the books for that. They sent letters to the leading rabbis in Jerusalem. Eventually I found out I couldn't. I am dead, according to Jewish law. But everyone is so understanding. And even though I pray at weird hours, the Jewish day starts at night, so I get a lot of community time in during the holy days.

Jewish stars, yes, and not crosses. I know, I know. I thought so too, Jew and vampire, the cross would melt me on the spot. But no, it's stars. And that's nice, because I have *Goyish* Vampire friends who can't go out sometimes, because everywhere they go there's a cross. And like I was saying before, the *Goyish* women, they get all dressed up for the clubs—and the clubs are the best place to find food—and then bam, last thing they throw on is a big shiny cross. But how many Jewish stars do you see? Even for me it's maybe twice a week. And silver doesn't do anything to me either. Not a thing. Do you know what does? And I don't make this up, but it's gold. Gold burns me. Jews and money you don't hear the end of and now the Jewish Vampire gets a better sense of the value of metal? But I don't control it. This is how it is.

Why would I become an orthodox Jew after all this? It's just . . . well, I don't know. But I'll tell you, I remember that the first thing that bothered me—really freaked me out—was when the foreskin grew back. Messed up isn't it? I mean, here I wake up in my bathroom in this pool of my own sticky mess and blood—and just starving, hungry like you should never know for blood, so that I'm licking the crust of it off of that cold tile floor—and I look down and there it is, like, like a—I mean, you know how it is, how it looks, right? How do they do that? Who wants that? I was so freaked out by that, not the fangs or the way sunlight hurt like a hot heat, but that. And it's there, I guess, it's right there when I started my journey back to traditional Judaism.

Now I just cut it off every eight days. It grows back in like an hour. But I figure eight days. Every one of us has one for that long anyway. But this is how I justify it. It's not out on a high mountain or across the sea that you can't do it. That's a quote from Talmud, I think. And it's true.

Robert P. Kaye

The Poison Hotline

Poison Hotline, Brad speaking, how can I help?

My husband's poisoning himself. He's emptied a whole bottle of habanero hot sauce on my tuna casserole. Any blander, he says, and he'd eat the placemat and hope to choke. That hurt my feelings.

Yeah. Ouch. It hurts to be unappreciated, I know. But please don't cry. What's your name?

Azalea.

Azalea—I need you to take a deep breath. That's it. Now exhale, and breathe normally. Where's your husband now?

At the table. He's red and sweating like, I don't know—a rainstorm? He's dripping sweat all over the table, panting like a dog and splattering bits of noodle everywhere, like a tuna noodle rainstorm.

Azalea, he'll be fine. Give him some milk or yogurt to neutralize the peppers. And next time, put a little spice in the casserole, because we all need a little heat in our lives.

Is that true? Do you like hot food?

I used to, but there's a lot of stress in my life right now and spices don't agree with my stomach anymore.

• • •

Poison Hotline, Brad speaking, how can I help?

Passaik, Jack Passaik—like the city in New Jersey, but with a K. I've been poisoned by plastic.

Tell me what happened, Mr. Passaik.

The mail's what happened, full of credit card offers. For years, I ripped them up and paid cash or did without, but then I'm thinking, what the hell? I'm old, might as well die in debt, right? So I buy the plasma TV, the Blu-ray, even the computer I can't figure out how to use, all on the plastic. Then the pool table, because I always wanted a pool table, right?

Right. So now you're in debt?

They jacked the rates after the swimming pool. Pool table, swimming pool—logical, right? These loan sharks toss their cards in the water like chum and soon as a sucker bites, bang!, it's Frenzyville. Worst of all, I'm nowhere close to dead.

Mr. Passaik, cut up the plastic and throw it in the trash. Don't open any more card offers. You can get out of this.

Can I keep the pool table?

Sure. You have to stay active. Sit in a little room all day with no windows and you start to die. I know all about that.

And the swimming pool? It's a big hole in the ground, right? Hard to return.

Sure. But turn the heat down.

• • •

Poison Hotline, Brad speaking. How can I help?

Brad, this is Stephanie. Are you a doctor?

Afraid not. Has someone been poisoned there?

Yes—by his mother, is my guess. My fiancé is allergic to cake.

And he's eaten some cake?

Yes and no. He thinks it's deadly—birthday cake, retirement party sheet cake, get-down-on-one-knee-and-propose chocolate decadence cake; wedding cake the most lethal of all. So I made him a trifle—since he's trifling with my affections? He scarfs it down. I point out that trifle is cubes of cake and he spits it out and leaves. He may call you in a bit.

I doubt it. Sounds like you already know you need a new fiancé.

Do you ever date callers, Dr. Brad?

I never date anyone—especially callers. I'd lose my job.

Is your job that great anyway?

It's hell on earth, Stephanie. But I love it.

• • •

Poison Hotline, Brad speaking. Have you been poisoned?

Does exposure to mindless bureaucracy count?

Is that you, Norm?

Yeah, Brad. How you doing today?

The usual. I woke up dreaming that I ate a bowl full of gravel like breakfast cereal. Found a tooth chip in my mouth.

Damn, Brad. Well. I said I'd call after the budget meeting. They yanked our funding, so we're done at the end of the year.

But who will people call when we're gone?

Not our problem, come January. Look, we both know most of them will be fine, and this is killing us.

Sure. Funny thing is, I'm not sure what I'll do without them. What if I need them more than they need me? What if—

Brad, I need you to take a deep breath. That's it. You clear out your desk at the end of this shift and don't come back. Get a jump on finding that new job. Your salary's covered until January. Brad? Still there?

Yeah, Norm. I feel better already. Thanks.

Sure, man. Just breathe normally. You're going to be okay.

Kathy Fish

Delivery

The doorbell rang. It was an older gentleman wearing a tuxedo, a bundle in his arms.

"Package for you," he said, handing it over.

"It's a baby," Mabel said. Its wee mouth gaped, emitting an odd, churring sound, like a hummingbird.

The man smiled. "A newborn," he said.

She held the bundle out in front of her. The swaddling came loose. The infant burped. "I was expecting a vintage radio. I didn't order this."

"We had to make a substitution."

"I don't even like babies. The whole motherhood thing . . ." Mabel shuddered.

The thing was unwieldy. Mabel held it out to the man. It slipped out of its blankets and fell to the floor.

Mabel and the tuxedoed gentleman stared. The infant yowled.

"Are you going to pick it up?" Mabel asked.

"Not in my job description. I do deliveries." The man clasped his hands behind his back, yawed to the right and to the left like a metronome. The infant screamed. Mrs. Yeardley, Mabel's next-door neighbor, stared from the sidewalk. Her annoying little dog, Huntley, yapped.

"Is there a problem?" Mrs. Yeardley called, but got no response.

"Oh for God's sake," Mabel said. She picked up the baby and hoisted it over her shoulder. "This is obviously a mistake."

"I'm very good with babies," Mrs. Yeardley called, a little louder. The man turned and held his hand up to her.

"All's well here," he said. "Just a little adjustment phase. It's quite normal. Go on about your business."

Mabel patted the infant on the bottom, bounced on her knees, swung from side to side. Still, it cried, its damp cheek against her own. The man in the tuxedo was saying something but it was difficult to make out.

"I should get a what? A nine-volt battery? Is that what you said? Come back here!"

The man was already down the steps and unlatching the gate. He turned and smiled. "Well," he said. "Enjoy."

The infant settled lumpily against Mabel's breast. "You smell like oatmeal," Mabel said. She pinched its nose and twisted it. "You are not a vintage radio. Not even close."

Robert Vaughan

The Three Stooges Explain Relativity

Shoebox (Larry)

We go on like this for days until we have a shoebox of memories. Okay, a shoebox of aches, like we'd graduated with the highest temperatures in our class. Easier to cremate the remains. *Creamation*, she calls it. When it's overflowing we carry the shoebox to Chinatown. Along the way she says, "Every time you think, you weaken the nation." I didn't wanna say yes, but I couldn't say no. So I stay quiet. We sell it to Jin Lee for a song and a dance. He chooses "God Bless America" while doing a jig. I laugh while she bobs around. Jin Lee asks me, "Were you born in this country? And I say, "No, Milwaukee."

Spies (Moe)

"Paranoid? Who, me? What's the big idea?"

The soda jerk gets on my nerves, says I need therapy just because I'm suspicious of everything: Mabel's bowling nights, government boondoggles, my neighbor Lipschitz whose mutt craps on my lawn. I catch Lipschitz spying on me, peeking through the moth holes in his curtains like I'm some dangerous nut.

"C'mon," says the jerk, "what's'a'matter witcha'? You think the whole world's out to getcha."

His ice cream scoop is just out of my reach, or I'd clonk his coconut to see how hollow it sounds. "I'm telling ya, da knucklehead's dang video camera points at our house non-stop. I'd like to stick that thing up where he keeps his head most of the time."

"Aah, you're all wet."

"Wise guy, huh?" I tweak his nose real good. Boink!

"Ow! I didn't do nuttin'!"

"That's in case you do when I ain't around."

He rubs his nose with an ice cube. "You know, my bowling night's the same as Mabel's."

"Remind me to murder you later," I say, spreading two fingers as far apart as his eyes.

Sidebar (Curly)

Around that time I was just crazy about Spanish food . . . especially corned beef and cabbage. I thought most everyone should play bocce. One time we played at camp and I was hooked. My parents bought a set. This was before my father died dancing, on the end of a rope. I trained the neighborhood kids, some parents, too. Then I started them tournaments. People paid to enter, and winners took all. Poifect! The local paper ran a story about my enterprise and soon other tourneys cropped up around town. My grades tanked. We're not ordinary people, we're morons. Neighbors threatened to sue. I thought I'd rather be dead, but there's no future in it. They'd sneer, "Nyuk, Nyuk, Nyuk" in my face. Finally, mom sold the bocce set. It was all gone except the smaller ball. I hid that in the cherry tree.

DINTY W. MOORE

REVOLUTION

Half-awake, I stumble into the kitchen to a symphony of slow belching noises blasting from the coffeemaker, my tired brain ticking off the list of chores that will inevitably ruin my weekend: clean the gutters, wash the porch, fix the wobbly table, replace the Mr. Coffee.

Outside, I hear the Saturday morning drone of neighborhood lawnmowers and remember one more errand: the lawnmower repair shop. I consider just turning around, retreating to bed, when I hear a slight, insistent knocking at my door.

"Wait a minute," I call.

But my neighbor Mort just barges in.

"Good news," he shouts. Mort wears a red T-shirt that doesn't quite reach the waistband of his orange corduroy shorts. His tummy pokes out, like a hunk of raw turkey breast.

"Mort," is all I manage to say.

"Really good news." Mort's left hand runs over his thin yellow hair. His T-shirt rides up his belly a bit further, rests on the shelf below his breasts. For a moment, he looks panicked.

"Mort," I say. "Spit it out."

"Okay! I'm not mowing *my* lawn either. Been studying your front yard, all weedy, all *au naturel*, and, damn it Ham, I'm doing the same." He pauses, pulls himself up straight. "I told Wendy this morning."

"Mort," I say. "My lawnmower . . ."

He winks. "Hell, Hamilton, I've told everyone. The guys are psyched. Totally. It's a brave thing you've done. A far braver thing than ... than whatever."

"Mort."

He stops, grins. "This is big, Hammer-man. This is about more than just crabgrass and dandelions."

"What are you talking about?"

"Evolution! Like that Beatles song . . ."

"Which Beatles song?"

"Listen! What do we husbands do all day, every day? We sit at desks, wear ties, grow hemorrhoids, while some jerk-off yells at us because our TPS report is incomplete. Well a tie is just a polyester noose, you know that, Hambone?" Mort mimics a man being strangled, his arm holding the rope, his tongue lolling out of the left side of his mouth. "Then we come home, and our wives pick up the slack. 'Mow the lawn,' and we mow. 'Take out the trash,' and we drag plastic sacks out the door as fast as our chubby old legs can carry us. 'Spend time with little Junior,' and we hit the floor making truck noises and getting rug lint on our good clothes. We're like trained dolphins at the circus, the ones that ride bikes and balance balls on their noses."

"I think those are seals, Mort."

"Men used to be men, Hamilton. We'd frolic in the woods, eat live chickens with our teeth. We did as we pleased, whenever we pleased."

"And?" Mort is an odd guy, even for a neighbor.

"And I'm gonna grow me a splendidious jungle, set a lawn chair right dead in the middle. At night I'll light torches." Mort's eyes flare. "I've got these Kon-Tiki jobbers that Wendy made me buy, and we never use 'em because who the hell can we invite for a picnic? And, Ham . . ."

"What?"

"You gotta know this." My neighbor gets teary-eyed, throws his pale pudgy arms around my neck. "You've saved my damn life. Just this brief talk between guys, regular guys, has made me feel so emasculated."

"Emancipated, Mort."

He doesn't hear.

Instead, Mort turns, springs through my door, hops down the rotting front steps, dances a jig on my small front patch of untended turf. He seems pretty happy, and for just a moment, I envy the guy.

And then, as if on signal, all the mowers in the neighborhood sputter off at once.

Bob across the street grins and waves in my direction.

Ed crosses his arms, stands at attention.

Dick, on the far corner, salutes.

Tania Hershman

The Google 250

The Google 250. Him and 249 others. The most searched-for. So they took them into hiding. Most of them women, the famous ones, the ones you knew every curve, every smile. And him, because of his money. They flew them all to an island, somewhere, who knows where. "You'll be safe here," they said. "Ain't no paparazzi, ain't no one that we don't say can come here." He breathed out.

From that day on, whenever someone with coffee-shop fever, surfing at one of those terminals, with less brain than porridge, Googled one of them, the authorities sent the Googler a warning, harshly worded, "for your own safety." There were complaints, of course, everyone moaning, "but I need to know what he/she is . . .!" The authorities didn't care. This was what had to be done.

On the island, no one was getting by very well. The most-Googled didn't know what to do with one another. People were having dreams about browser pages that had words missing, their names had wings and took flight, like heads off a goldfish. They felt like they were disappearing. He was watching one of the women, a film star, more beautiful for her proximity, all soft skin and perfect teeth. He watched her as they breakfasted together, in the communal dining room. I can see why they Googled her, he thought, over bran flakes. I would Google her too, I would Google her right now. She's got nothing to hide, he decided. But he did, now. He had something to hide called desire.

One day, after lunch prepared by that surly most-Googled British chef, he slid up behind the movie star. "I would," he whispered to her. She turned, surprised, her face frozen into annoyance at the intrusion. But then she saw him, knew him from the media, and she opened towards him. "You would . . .?" she said, and he saw that he was allowed to lead her by the arm back to his quarters.

There, he mimed switching on the laptop he didn't have, and she shivered in anticipation. He acted out opening Google.com and she giggled; he pretended to enter her name and teased her by holding back from pressing Enter. "Do it, do it!" she cried, throwing her head back, showing him her long, pale neck. "Oh God, just do it!" He pressed Enter, she began to moan, and together they watched the phantom search results roll in.

Barry H. Leeds

Not the Bend Over Part

After receiving recommendations for perhaps a dozen lawyers, ranging in style and appearance from Mike Hammer (picture an ex-cop who arrives with a hangover, tosses his hat at the rack and misses, and opens his desk drawer to reveal a pint of Old Cirrhosis and a loaded .38) to Clarence Darrow, I had my appointment with Sean Seamus O'Reilly.

After my initial upset at Rhonda's preemptive strike in engaging Attorney John Peepers, grandson of Wally Peepers and cousin to Fred Rogers, I decided to give her a little history lesson. If she ever reads another book outside of *Fifty Shades of Grey*, I suggest it be a history of all those who underestimated their adversaries, to their eternal dismay and detriment. In the immortal words of that arrogant popinjay George Armstrong Custer, "Where the fuck did all these Indians come from?"

With my folder of Splitsville documents already an inch thick and growing, armed with a six-page summary of the marriage and finances, I went to meet O'Reilly in the Glasscock Building downtown. He slouched and stomped into his ritzy office, 6'6" and 300 plus pounds of gin-blossomed, beer-bellied Irishman. I think he became a lawyer because he was too big and foul-mouthed to be a stevedore.

"I won't blow smoke up your ass, Frank. Mandrake the Magician probably couldn't keep you from having to bend over and take it like a man. But if you are going to get sodomized, at least I'll be honest about it. And I don't care what thimble-dick she gets, from any top law firm, I'm not afraid of *anyone* in court."

Despite the AC's arctic blast, my thighs stuck to the leather chair. "That's encouraging, I guess. Well, not the bend over part."

"Look, I'm used to defending criminals, handling malpractice cases, that sort of shit. You know, *real* lawyering, not like marital attorneys. Those pussies spend their time schmoozing in corridors and would piss their pants if they had to go before a judge to fight a case in court."

O'Reilly toyed with his hulking pinky ring, but the finger was too obese for it to budge. "I especially hate those bitchy, castrating divorce lawyers—and they're not all women. They remind me of my expensive wife."

"You should meet Rhonda Imelda Marcos Blank."

"Oh, don't you worry, pal. I'm going to meet her all right."

I thought of the hunting and weapons magazines inhabiting O'Reilly's waiting room, where I discovered that *Playgun* has a Piece of the Month centerfold. The closest thing to a women's magazine out there was *Field & Stream*. I suspected that his clients were almost exclusively possessors of Y chromosomes.

Next to this guy, I was a contender for the Clint Eastwood Taciturnity Award. Cracking his knuckles one at a time, O'Reilly gave me his "three-minute summary" of divorce law:

"In the 13th Century these guys used to wear iron suits . . ."

"By the 14th Century, these had started to rust . . ."

"The Black Death had a lighter side . . ."

"The Pope, a real bastard of a Borgia, issued an edict . . ."

After 45 minutes, he was up to 1776 and the impact of English Common Law upon the colonies. I'd have been comatose from boredom if not for O'Reilly's extortionate hourly rate, and the o-dough-meter spinning madly in my head.

O'Reilly leaned back in his enormous armchair. "To quote the lovely and talented Rob Reiner, 'But hey, enough of my yakking.' You've seen *Spinal Tap*, haven't you, Frank? It's an art house film. OK, let's hear *your* three minutes."

I was starting to hemorrhage money and have broad daylight nightmares about displacement, poverty, loneliness. But most of all, I didn't want to lose to someone who had begun channeling Leona Helmsley.

"I just have one question," I said before starting my three-minute saga that I knew would inevitably stretch into an hour.

O'Reilly aimed a pistol finger at my mangled heart. "Shoot."

"Do you validate parking?" I asked, iron resolve underpinning each quiver in my voice.

Zac Finkenstein

The Young Man and the D

He was a young man, who had sat alone at the desk in his dorm room, and he had gone eighty-four hours now without writing a word. In the first few hours his roommate had been with him for moral support. But after two days without a thesis statement the roommate's girlfriend had said that the young man was definitely and finally screwed, and the roommate had gone at her orders to Harry's, where they would down many shots and forget about classes.

There was an open window in the room. The young man looked outside as he did not write. Below was the festival of the Running of the Virgins. The *nombre oficial* was The Gamma Gamma Sorority Pledge Annual Cross-Campus Marathon, but everyone in the dorm called it the Running of the Virgins, and so that was how the young man thought of it. He was *muy aficionado* of the tight T-shirts, and of the short shorts as well. And a true *aficionado* of those who wore them, and they pulled his eyes from the blank screen the way a fisherman, or a writer, might feel a tug on a line. It was very good, but it was also very bad. Why did this have to be the one day all month that it hadn't rained?

You must concentrate, he thought. Everything will be good again, and you will find a thesis that is strong, and true, and precise, as the *viejo profesor* said a thesis should be. Yes, all will be good, if you just do not look out the obscene window again.

He looked out the obscene window. He was only on the second floor and he could see them breathe and stretch before the race. The blonde one up front was very fine. You are killing me, blonde, the young man thought. But you have the right pair. Never have I seen greater, or more beautiful. He was mesmerized by the topography of her shirt. Everything comes down to topography, he thought. She had hills like white elephants.

He knew now he would never write his thesis today, or finish the math problems due the next morning, or any of the other things that he had put off doing as long as they could be put off. That was over now. It was best not to think about it, he thought. He turned off the light in the room and headed out. Maybe she was an English major. And maybe she was one of those bitches who ruined the endings of movies you had not seen, and would tell him what happened in that novel he had not yet got around to reading. And maybe she would rattle off a thesis statement while doing her warm-up jumping jacks, and then she would write it for him in the nude, and he would get an A and not have to make up some bullshit tomorrow at the last moment.

"Yes," he said aloud, "isn't it pretty to think so?"

Matthew Charles

This City

Her bedroom smells like lilacs and poppy seeds, even though I'm pretty sure I don't know what a poppy seed smells like. Something like bagels, I guess. And maybe it isn't lilacs. It might be petunias or wildflowers or rhododendrons. The point is, it smells like flowers and bagels.

She has a small cat that stares at me from underneath the coffee table as I pass by with her feet dragging on the floor. Now is a good time to tell you that I didn't hit her over the head like a caveman looking for a wife and I didn't drug her like a seedy college kid looking for a bright future in the penal system. She had too much to drink at dinner and now I have spatters of vomit on my shoes and a slurring girl in my arms. And a judgmental cat to deal with.

I put her in bed, or rather on top of her bed, and she mumbles something into the pillow that may have been a thank you or may have been a protest because the pillow is stopping her from being able to breathe. I push her onto her side to be safe and put a wastebasket by the bed. But the basket is wicker, so I hope she doesn't actually get sick again.

"Come to bed," she says.

"I wish I could stay, darling," I tell her, brushing a strand of blonde hair away from her eyes. "But this city needs me. There are criminals that need to see justice and, with the way the courts work around here, they need me to do things that the law can't. I wear a suit and punch criminals. And sometimes I set off smoke bombs."

It sounds strange being said aloud, but really I never thought about it before now. It seems so normal when you're out there in your suit, scaring petty criminals and hanging gangsters and thugs from their feet ten stories up. It does sound a little absurd, though. I admit that.

"I love you," she says. I think.

"And I love this city. Take some aspirin when you wake up and drink plenty of water."

My suit is vomit-free, which is nice. I don't want to have to send her a dry cleaning bill.

I leave her in the bed, snoring and smelling of shrimp scampi and bile. I take off my dinner suit in her living room, exposing my crime-fighting suit underneath. I slide my mask on and leave my dinner tie looped on her doorknob in case she forgets me. The cat hisses a warning as I walk by and I hiss back, then climb out the window to go catch bad guys.

Louise Farmer Smith

VITA 1985

Once I quit crack, I had to get out of the CIA. Nothing made sense. I started a lawn business. Hedge clippers, weed whackers—the noise kept my head on. Unfortunately, my former contact showed up, thinking this was a cover. I wrote him a year's contract—mowing, trimming, fertilizer. He thought it was code and fed the numbers to the Chinese. They made a missile shield and paid me like crazy.

I branched out—annuals, gravel, landscaping. The Pakistanis wanted a piece and Tehran piled in, both using aerial photographs of my clients' yards. Ultraviolet transmogrifications produced state-of-the-art early warning systems. I was proud—three countries taking their coordinates off my zinnia borders.

Everything was coming up roses until the gopher infestation. Tehran bombed Canada, and my only option was to rejoin the Agency. Fortunately my old pusher still ran personnel.

Terry DeHart

Negotiations

Dear God:

I know You're on the receiving end of six billion people, give or take, always asking for shit, so please forgive me, but help!

Help me, help me, HELP! ME! One so lowly as me. You notice the fall of a single sparrow. Do you care that Big John put out a *contract* on my ass?

What can I do to get you on my side? How does eternal gratitude grab You?

Complete devotion for the rest of my life? You drive a hard bargain but okay, it's a deal.

Dear God:

It seems ridiculous to write to a dude who knows everything, but You've given me so many problems that I want to list a couple of them here, for the record.

First off, could You arrange it so Pauly Two-Toes doesn't pull the shotgun I know he's carrying in that flower box? I'd really appreciate it.

Dear God:

Well, I see You didn't intervene with the Pauly Two-Toes/shotgun thing. Also, Big Petey just walked into my office, too. He's got a blowtorch. I think he's about to light it. I'm asking for some divine intervention here, God.

I'm serious about the eternal devotion thing. And here's the sweet part of the deal: I'll throw in twenty percent of everything I make. Twenty percent of EVERYTHING—before the skim and the payoffs and Big John's take. I'll give it anonymously to my diocese. Deals don't get any better than that.

Dear God:

You crack me up. Bless You for making Big Petey's blowtorch explode in his face when he tried to light it. Bless You for causing Pauly Two-Toes to drop his shotgun. Bless You for causing the shotgun to go off and change Pauly's name to "Pauly Stumps." The guys who wrote the Holy Scriptures should've warned us about Your sense of humor. I just about passed a Danish through my nose when that shit happened.

Dear God:

I know it's been a while since I've written. About the money I owe you—I ran the numbers and I figure you had a reason to send Big Petey to hell and to maim Pauly Stumps. I figure I played an important part in your plans, and so it's only fair that I get some kind of reward. Am I right?

The amount I'm thinking of is in the mid-six-figure range. I'm only tacking on a two-point vig since we're such great buddies.

Dear God:

I was only kidding about You owing me money. If You allow me to escape from these pissed-off Yakuza Ninjas, I'll tear up my latest contract and honor our original agreement.

Dear God:

Here's the money I owe You, with interest. Thank You for allowing the re-attachment surgery to work out. The doctors say it's a miracle. I don't normally pay protection money, but hey, I'm a big-hearted guy. What can I say? Take the money. Enjoy. Salud!

Sincerely,
Sammy (Ginsu-Pecker) Torino

Scott Lambridis

The Pile

After one insult too many in the courtroom, the defendant removed a smuggled pistol, and the public defender, a brave and selfless man, jumped on top of him, and then the defendant's brother jumped on top of the public defender to wrench him off, and then someone else from the prosecution jumped on too, trying to stop the brother trying to stop the public defender trying to stop the shooter.

It happened so quickly, mere seconds, and then, sure enough, there was another on top, some oblivious juror who seemed to believe four men grabbing at each other must be a game, and then another who saw five men on the floor like that and called it obscene before jumping on to break it up, then another who feared a mob was forming, another making his first citizen's arrest, another who wanted the one on the bottom dead whoever the hell he was, another who recognized the resale value of that buried pistol, another who figured ten men together like that means paperwork anyway, another whose lucky number was twelve, another who was tired of always transcribing and never being involved, another because thirteen is bad luck, another who wondered if he'd missed a rugby game while he was in the bathroom, another who always hated being picked last in kickball, another who missed his many brothers, another who had been suicidal for some time but could never finish her note, another who'd been after workman's comp for some time, another whose training instinct said there's a bomb and it takes twenty bodies to really cover the blast, another who shouted "blackjack" when he pounced, another who never passed up even the most absurd business opportunities, another because there might be a reward, another who simply couldn't help himself, another who did everything "for the people" and her estranged father who always said the state comes first, another who got carried away with women's lib, another who wanted to be the plaintiff in a sexual harassment suit, another who believed orders are orders even if he didn't hear them, another who was paid good money to protect his supervisor's weak little spine, another who was that man's secret lover, another who didn't want to be caught looking stupid, another whose hatred of being a follower was only surpassed by his desire to understand all points of view, another who never wanted to be caught on the wrong side of a revolution again, another who was agoraphobic, another who loved social experiments, another whose doctor told him human contact alone could cure his analgesia, another because thirty-eight Swedes tried something similar in the Guinness book and dammit she wanted a record of her own, another who thought he could touch the ceiling, and even the bailiff, just to be sure we all stayed put until the authorities arrived.

Really, officer, there are so many ways to end up in a pile.

JESS CHAREST

MOUSE

The dead mouse was discovered in the filter of the swimming pool, right before the 6 A.M. polar bear swim-time. The Girl Scouts were up in arms.

"How could you let this happen?" They accosted the lifeguard, the only male human on camp premises. There was a mixed-race shepherd dog, also male, but he was far too innocent for such a crime. They called him Brownie, even though his real name was Arthur, and he hated to be called Brownie.

Most of the girls had never witnessed a dead thing before. Maybe a fish, or a Japanese beetle, but never anything as substantial (or soft) as this mouse. They were very sheltered children. Many of them were denied access to cable television.

"That little mouse is in Heaven now," they told each another.

"Death is so unpredictable," they whispered at flag ceremony.

For breakfast there were waffles with chocolate chips inside. Usually this was their favorite, but hardly any of the girls ate. The cook felt deflated. She worked very hard at her job, preparing healthy and delicious meals. Blue fish sticks, pancakes in the shape of hearts. She found mice in her kitchen almost every morning, and crushed them with her heavy Danish clogs.

After they did the dishes, the Girl Scouts were turned loose in the field, and they ran around wildly, chasing the dog, trying to grab on to his tail. Arthur tired of this quickly, and retreated to his secret place in the woods, where he had stockpiled a collection of rabbit corpses.

The girls were out of breath. They sat in the grass and discussed the tragedy of the mouse. Some were in favor of burial, others argued for cremation.

"I wonder if we'll get a badge for this," Allison said softly.

The thought had crossed all of their minds.

Rand Richards Cooper

El Turista

So here it is, the low moment in the life of a travel writer, the absolute nadir: you've spent ten days in the Colonial Heartland of Mexico, touring four cities, tasked with evoking their ambience and architecture and history and cuisine—in 2000 words—by an editor who *absolutely adores* this region and is steering you to every marketplace food stall and artisan's workshop, every soldier-priest's memorial, every last barroco curlicue of stone in every Franciscan convent courtyard, so you can *really do it justice!*; and you're on your last night in the silver-mining city of Zacatecas, at the *fabulous* hotel in the *amazing* ex-bullring where last night you snorted down multiple Herredura-and-sangritas to ease the constant hotel-hopping and drown a flicker of paranoia lit by rumors of recent tourist abductions, and where the magazine turns out to have succeeded in booking not two nights but one only, a snafu that leaves you competing for a room tonight against a big group in town this week, *los charros*, the rodeo riders, as the concierge at his desk has just now managed to convey to you, twirling an invisible lasso while he phones around to other hotels, and you meanwhile silently monitor an intestinal agitation surely traceable to tap water ingested yesterday at that same rodeo, in the form of tequila-accompanying ice cubes whipped up from some fetid barrio culvert, your intestine gurgling an SOS as you wonder what happened to the dream of becoming a great travel writer, the next Naipaul or Theroux or Orwell, and the concierge informs you, sadly hanging up the phone, that there's no room anywhere in town, though wherever you rest tonight, you will rest well, *Señor*, because he's sending someone to drive you to the airport at 4:30 A.M., someone especial, is no problem, is completely safe, is named El Gato, *si, Señor,* like the cat, and on and on until finally there's nothing left but to beat a retreat to your room, waves of self-pity drenching you in loathing for this so-called Colonial Heartland with its insane cathedral facades and howling mariachi bands, in fact, for this entire smog-choked, machismo-besotted, superstitious, corrupt and reeking country, where nothing gets done, and thieves cross themselves in front of churches, and dogs die unloved in the street, and histrionic teen romances subside into sham marriages—just as you, who once set out to write *The Road to Wigan Pier*, have subsided into describing foie gras-stuffed ancho chilis and hibiscus enchiladas: you, travel journalist, peon, pathetically shoveling your chunk of coal into the roaring blast furnace of American leisure; and while these bitter thoughts are unworthy of you, perhaps, they are the thoughts of a man still unaware that he has reached the absolute nadir, the low point from which your trip will magically recover: unaware, that is, that your stomach will survive; that you will succeed in finding a room for the night, at a spartan but wholly functional hotel on the main plaza; that at sunset a band will strike up a dreamy Victor Herbert waltz on the plaza, where a café table and chair will offer up a prime seat and soothing glass of chilled *Xtabentún*; and that tomorrow morning at 4:30, when you wheel your suitcase out to the dark street, a man with a car will be waiting—El Gato himself, as promised!—so that you will repent of having thought that nothing gets done in this country, gladly paying the man a hundred pesos for the twenty-minute ride to the airport: during which, while scooting through pitch-black desert, he will turn out the lights at a railroad crossing and stop the car to peer both ways along the tracks; and in that moment when the lights go off, radiant full moon hanging to your left, hills rising to your right, landscape like black velvet sheened everywhere in silver, it will be as if the deep geology of the place has risen up to make art, truly a silver city in a silver world, and in the quiet you will chuckle from sheer delight—knowing that this one moment, with its hints of the sublime, is worth the entire trip, and that you're going to get this moment in, the moon and the silver and El Gato too, and make it editor-proof, welding it to everything else with infernal slyness, so that try as she might with her surgeon's pencil, she will not be able to cut it out.

Steven Ostrowski

Willard

A guy I know because, get this, we were in the same Lamaze class years ago (with our wives, I mean), and who I had not laid eyes on since, so he comes into the dumpy coffee house near the river where I'm working until I can find something less humiliating. It's not until he gets to the counter that his name comes back to me: Willard. Like the rat in that old movie. He looks older than he did in the Lamaze days, grayer, face more sunken, nose longer, ears hairier, but I know right off the bat it's him.

—Holy shit, he says to me. I know you. Um . . .

—Trevor. And you're Willard. 'Breath in, breath out.' Remember?

We look at our feet, chuckle.

—Long gone, he says. The wife, I mean. Not dead gone. New-freakin'-husband gone. He owns this fancy cheese shop, you know? How's yours? Amanda, was it? Had that sexy way of breathing.

—Had *what?*

—Nothing, nothing. How's the wife?

—She's gone, too. Cosmic midwife out in California.

—Midwife? What's that, a part-time wife? Half a wife? Probably legal in California.

—No, she delivers babies for women who don't trust doctors to do it.

—I delivered a kitten once, Willard says. Well, not really. Just watched. Anyway, how you doing, um . . .?

—Trevor. I spread my arms out, like, look at me. Fifty-two. Wearing an apron. Cleaning crumbs off unbalanced plastic tables. —What do you do, Willard?

—Still in pest control. Mice and squirrels mostly.

—You get rid of rats?

He looks at me sideways, like it's a dirty joke.

—We got rats out back. Big suckers with bad attitudes. Hey, want a cup of joe? Mocha? Espresso? On me.

—No fancy shit. Plain coffee. One cream and lots of sugar. I like it sweet.

I start dumping sugar into a cardboard cup and wait for his sign to stop, but he don't give me one. Finally I stop anyway.

—Twenty years ago, he says, that Lamaze business. More. What's your kid doing now?

—Not much. He don't live in this country.

—No shit.

—He's up in Greenland.

—*Greenland?* That's the one that's all ice, right? Iceland is green and Greenland is ice, right? What's he do?

—Sharpens skates.

—No, seriously.

—I'm serious. Never mind. What about your boy?

Willard gulps some coffee. —Trying to make it as a sit-down comic.

—Don't you mean stand-up comic?

He holds the cup in both hands. —Joey fell off a balcony at a wedding and paralyzed his legs. So now he calls himself a sit-down comic.

—Maybe he becomes famous, huh?

—Maybe. Except he tells *anti*-jokes.

—What the hell's an anti-joke?

—Knock knock.

Before I can say "Who's there?" Willard goes —It's open.

—What?

—That's it. That's the joke.

—God bless him, I say.

—God can bless him by getting him on Letterman. Right now he's the opening act at Lucky's Gentlemen's Club, for some bald pervert who juggles flaming dildos.

—Yikes. That coffee sweet enough, Willard?

—You went a little crazy with the sugar. So your boy's in Iceland, huh? Sharpening skates.

—Greenland.

—Okay, so what'd the wife say to the husband?

—Hmm. 'Honey, we have to talk.'

—No. She didn't say nothing. They're both married to somebody else.

—Oh.

—I don't get it either, but everything's like that now. No plot, no punch line. He says he's 'growing' an audience. Man, I hope so.

Willard looks depressed as hell, so I say --Try one more on me. Maybe anti-jokes grow on you.

He sighs. —Why'd the llama fall out of the tree?

I shut my eyes. —Was it icy up there?

—No, the friggin' thing was dead.

I'm thinking, poor llama. Up in a tree where he don't belong, dies, falls out. That has to suck. But Willard's waiting for my reaction.

—Yeah, I get it, I say. The llama's dead. Ha!

I start to laugh—really laugh—and so does Willard.

Picture it: the two of us standing there laughing like jackasses. Laughing so hard we're crying.

Leslie Rapparlie

Interview

Thank you for coming and please take a seat so we can begin. Were you waiting long? You were early so it isn't our fault, but being prompt is a desirable trait and I've made a note of it in your file.

I assume you're aware of the position's responsibility? Some of the duties include inputting data into the company's software. You are familiar with the program? While the posting says that we offer training for things such as this, we prefer not to because it costs money. Not that we're cheap.

Do you prefer to work alone or in a team environment? If you read the job posting you will know the answer we want.

You'll notice that I'm writing as you speak but don't worry, I'm just taking notes to remember what you're saying—it's mandatory. Although, your last answer was relatively boring, so I drew a cat instead. I'm actually very good at drawing cats. And bulldozers, oddly.

How do you feel about working evenings and some weekends? This position requires that, so if you want the job, you can't mind it. They say that interviews go both ways and candidates are also interviewing employers, but I've never seen that happen. No one has ever walked out when I've told them we pay them for forty hours a week but often ask them to work many more. No one has ever asked me a question.

What are your three greatest strengths? Please don't say hardworking. Everyone says hardworking. Also, name one area where you can improve. "Nothing" or "I don't know" are not options.

Rate yourself on a scale from one to ten, ten being the highest. If you don't rate yourself above a seven, you will not be invited to the next round of interviews. If you rate yourself a ten, the same thing will happen. Be honest.

Have you ever stolen from a previous employer? This is not limited to money. A pencil? A stapler? Remember that we have a list of your references and will call to verify this.

We have a zero tolerance policy on stealing as one year we spent double our supply budget on pens and Post-its that went missing. Now each employee uses a different color Post-it pad to avoid this. If you had to pick a color, what would it be?

I've made a note of that in your file, next to the drawing of the cat.

I've only looked at the clock once so far, which is a good sign because usually I'm checking it every few minutes. I make candidate recommendations to the president tomorrow, then I can finally get back to my regular work. Interviewing is just added to all my usual responsibilities and I don't get compensated for it, although I'm not supposed to tell you that.

Our insurance company requires that we ask if you're active. If you are, you'll get a discount on local gyms from the provider and also be invited to participate, along with the rest of us, in company weight loss competitions and in races where we raise money for various causes. We all wear T-shirts to the event with the winner's name on them. It builds morale. This, along with other benefits, will be explained in a handout during orientation, if you're invited.

How is your handwriting? Please provide a sample here.

Yes, right there, under the dotted line.

I will check my email while I wait for you to finish.

I hope it takes you awhile.

That is the end of the questions on my form, which brings me to the discussion of salary. What do you hope to get paid? I will write this number in red on the top of your file, next to your name. If it is too high, your file will not make the next cut. If it is too low, you can expect to be offered exactly that amount, which will be your own fault.

Do you have any questions for me? It's important to have at least one question to show that you care about this position and company. The questions you ask will be recorded and part of your evaluation.

That's all the time we have. Thank you again for coming in. Another candidate will be arriving soon and we'd like to avoid any interaction between the two of you. Here's my card. Do not call us or you may be removed from consideration.

T.J. Coane

America's Got Smarts!

"Deuce Bigalow: Male Gigolo." *Right again. Another $1000 to you.* Of course I was right. Of course I knew the answer. Jared Pearce you ignorant dingus, you American treasure, why would you even say that? Oh right, because you're paid to make a little comment after every single answer. Paid more than I could ever hope to win on *America's Got Smarts!* even if I played for another ten years. Which I could. Well, in theory, anyway. I'd have a hard time continuing after blowing my brains out around year three.

"The capacity of the human rectum." You're paid to read, you ugly bastard. You probably get so much ass, too. And just because you're a perfect target for girls with daddy issues. They probably line up in front of your dressing room to have you correct their grammar. They wouldn't even wonder if you were wrong about something—and I bet you love that—because you make a living out of getting to correct people a hundred times smarter than you. I could answer a million questions and some people would still think you're smarter than me. One question wrong and I look like your bitch, chastised with a condescending, *Oh, so close, but no it's actually* Henry the Fourth, Part Two. Part *Two.*

"The Thong Song." Who's the jackass in this situation really, though? The putz who's reading the answer off a card, or the shmuck who actually knows what Sisqó's 1999 hit single was? That is actually in my head. I had to carve out a piece of my mind for that to nestle itself into.

"Deuce Bigalow: European Gigolo." Last week I had to call AAA when I got a flat tire. I don't know how to change a tire. I waited on the side of the highway for two hours. By the time I made it to my job, I didn't have it anymore. In the competitive world of data entry, if you're not there to enter data, there's the exit. I also don't know how to swim.

"K-E-dollar sign-H-A." I guess this is my job now, knowing how to spell every teen pop idol's stage name, both because it's the only thing I'm good at, and because it isn't fun so it's not a hobby. Though it doesn't even really feel like a job either. At least not any more than breaking a chair could be considered a fat guy's job. Like him, some of my organic material is just constructed in such a way that allows me to perform a spectacularly unhelpful feat. In my case, to store worthless information. I wish I had the fat guy's gig. At least he has something that can't be done a hundred times quicker and more accurately by a robot.

"Jesus Christ." Jesus Christ, where do they get these contestants? I'm crushing them. I could go out for a beer and still be ahead when I get back. Maybe I should try to get on *The Real World* instead. They have beer. Maybe they accept socially awkward 39-year-olds with a disturbing amount of back hair. Girls love back hair they can get tangled in, right? Now that I think about it, my back hair is kind of like trivia: the more I try to cut it away, the more ferociously it returns and stays with me. The more room it takes up, too. Did you know hair can grow on shoulders? That's one piece of information that actually would have been useful, at least so I could have mentally prepared myself. It's like I have shoulder pads. I guess I could talk about my body hair during the interview part of the show. They say it should be something you're passionate about.

"The World's Largest Ball of Dog Earwax." Some of this stuff glazing my brain isn't so bad, I guess. If I'm ever in Possum Tumble, Idaho I'll know exactly where to go to find the four-feet-high brownish-yellow ball of canine canal crud painstakingly collected, molded and cared for by Ms. Miriam Honeybucket Doubleday. Just as assuredly as I know the Aztec rain god is Tlaloc and not Chalchiuhtlicue like so many dumbasses think.

Just like I know it shouldn't take this long to microwave three burritos. Come on, I don't have all night!

"MA, WHERE'S MY DARN DINNER?"

Allen Woodman

World's Best Joke

A woman calls to break up with me, even though I don't know her. She dialed the wrong number. She says, "I don't know who I am anymore, but we just don't work."

I repeat her words, "I don't know who I am anymore," although I really do not know who she is.

She continues, "We love each other so much, but we can't go on this way."

"You have the wrong number," I tell her.

She laughs. "That is so like you. Can't face the truth."

On that, she has my number. "You're right, I can't face the truth."

I have had wrong number phone calls before, back when I was married. Once, our new phone number was the same as the defunct Jokeline.

People would call the old Jokeline number needing a joke-a-day, and I would answer. I'd try to tell them that they had the wrong number, but they'd say, "That's not funny."

After a while, I started to tell them jokes. I got a joke book from Barnes & Noble. I Googled jokes.

My wife was not amused. She would shake her head in disgust. When she got a wrong number call, she would hang up.

I knew that things were not good between us when she told me, right before bedtime, that the previous night she had dreamed of plunging scissors into my eyes while I slept. In her dream, I must have deserved it, she said. I think you can tell a lot about a person if they dream of stabbing you in the eyes in your sleep.

After reading *Eat, Pray, Love,* my wife left me. She wanted to be alone, she said, so she ran off to Italy with one of her co-workers. That day, I told callers on the Jokeline that I was the world's best joke.

The woman who dialed the wrong number is still talking between sobs, calling me her baby.

I try to think of something to help. I tell her a joke that according to Wikipedia was the funniest joke in the UK: "A woman gets on a bus with her baby. The bus driver says, 'That's the ugliest baby I've ever seen. Ugh!' The woman goes to the rear of the bus and sits down, fuming. She says to a man next to her, 'The driver just insulted me!' The man says, 'You go right up there and tell him off--go ahead, I'll hold your monkey for you.'"

I tell her another. I am on a roll like a giant wheel of humor, and she laughs, a sweeter laugh this time. "Stop it," she says, her voice softening, but I see the green light.

My wife always said that I was too chirpy for her, and she was right. Even now, alone, I wake up in the morning and make up silly songs to sing about my breakfast toast. And if someone calls and needs a joke, the optimist in me will give them a joke and think that somehow it might help.

I give the woman on the phone a quotation about misrepresentation. I say it in a soft voice, "Chico Marx said, 'I wasn't kissing her, I was just whispering in her mouth.'"

She gets quiet. I can almost feel her smiling inside. She starts talking about the history of our relationship, our first date, the sweet first kiss.

Giving me a halfway guilty look, Raymond the cat starts working on a hairball.

I wave my hand towards him like I am waving goodbye to something. "It's OK. Get it out," I say to both of them.

I think about my history with my ex-wife and how I thought that we would be together forever, and how now we would always be apart. I think about it as the woman on the phone talks about her story, until my story is like some other person's dream in my head.

"History has no future," I say, emboldened by the distance on the line. I know it's a bad joke, but it's also a kind of hope that there will be a new future, a new first kiss, a chance to live another life, and I wait in the silence, listening before action.

"You sound different," she says tenderly.

My tongue thickens. The past is slipping away. There will be things to work out when we meet, but anything can happen.

"I am different," I say. "I've changed. I am a new man."

Frances Lefkowitz

Dessert for Superman

Betty has been bench-pressing all morning, and she is finally ready for Superman. She strokes her own muscles, firm as metal, and hopes she and her man won't get into another tiff. He complains about a lot of things, but mostly he accuses her of not needing him enough. If only she frightened more easily, then she would be impressed by his do-good antics, the wingspan of his shoulder blades, the speed with which he changes into his cape. Last time he was over, she finally asked him about the fabric stretching across his chest, bright blue to emphasize bulging: was he perhaps addicted to too much adoration? They got into it, and she accused him of being knee-jerk American, not even pausing to question reports they read in the newspaper. "Wondering does not make me a Communist," she told him as they watched Animal Planet on television, some show about a species of ferocious sharks going extinct. He rose from the couch and slammed the door behind him, leaving his ice cream to dry and crust in the bowl. Betty didn't care who you were, you should have the forethought to place the bowl in the sink and fill it with water, to make the cleanup easier. She decided to let that bowl sit there on the floor and attract ants if that was what was necessary for a lesson to be learned. It was her bowl and her apartment, so she was the one who watched the fidgeting black stream trickle in, then gush. But still.

Next thing Betty knew he was calling her from Holland of all places. Superman has an iPhone. "I hate it here," he whined. "They don't know who I am." Which only proved her point, about the adoration. But need, from a man with shoulders like his, can be an aphrodisiac, especially from a distance. "Maybe you should come home," she told him. "What?" he said, begging for more encouragement. "Come home," she ordered him. She wanted to ask another question, but she couldn't risk upsetting him. But even after she hung up, she couldn't stop wondering about the extinction of the phone booth, if that's why he traveled overseas, or if there's an app for that.

Now, because he flies so extremely fast and arrives with every hair in place, he was almost here, and Betty had little time to tidy up. The ants were gone, having devoured the ice cream, having licked that bowl clean. No need to wash it; she would use it tonight to serve Superman his dessert.

David Partenheimer

Nude Noodling in Slovinger Missouri

Call me Dakota. I am a white, lesbian, suburban American with weight issues, and a recent graduate of Yale University in anthropology. I did not get a grant to pursue field studies in an important place like Africa, Nepal, Samoa, or the Amazon rainforest. Fortunately, a friend at Mullhouse University in Mullhouse, Missouri gave me a hot tip for a research project on the cheap. Not far from Mullhouse in the half town of Slovinger is an active cult of night noodlers. Noodling refers to the practice of catching fish with your bare hands. This ancient method of fishing is not unusual in itself, but the ritual of doing so in the nude at night requires academic research. Because it is restricted to a clandestine clan in Slovinger, I had to go undercover. I needed to win the trust of the natives by becoming one of them.

My friend at Mullhouse University headed me in the right direction. She dropped me off at a derelict bar named Gropos, where she pointed out the ringleader of lowlife from the area, Tom Bullock. Mr. Bullock is a resident noodler at the bar for girls. May I keep this part of my research report brief. I enjoyed his testimony on his personal relations with the sheep on his farm. Soon I will prepare a monograph about it within the larger context of early nomadic tribes before sexual taboos. In any case, I paid him a visit at his farm. I found the cacique nude, sitting on a lawn chair with his feet in a 300-gallon water trough and a beer can in each hand. My sleepover at the farm was traumatic, but I am receiving professional treatment and have joined a support group.

Mr. Bullock could not introduce me directly to the circle of noodlers in Slovinger, but he hooked me up with a resident with status, a man named PJ. Mr. PJ is not a practicing noodler himself, but a champion truck puller. This practice is widespread in impoverished rural areas throughout most of the United States. It consists of spending every penny in your pockets on souping up a truck that can pull a weight transfer sledge for a few feet along the sand until the motor burns up and catches on fire. Afterwards, the trucks are towed away, and the participants borrow more money or make meth in order to repair their trucks and pull again.

I was a truck pull groupie for three months. Once I won the trust of PJ, he introduced me to a local poacher, Kyler. He just went by his last name, Kyler. He had four brothers, who called themselves Kyler as well. Half the town of Slovinger has the name Kyler. In any case, Kyler got me into the poaching business and close to the Slimy River, the site of the noodling ritual. He dressed me up in camouflage, then placed me in a tree blind with a rifle to shoot a deer for dinner. I spent three full days in the tree looking for a deer to slaughter, but didn't see one.

On the third night, though, a procession of men and boys marched right beneath my tree blind. In the moonlight I could identify the subjects as noodlers because only the boys had all their fingers. Through serendipity, my wish and research objective had become reality. Furtively, I stumbled out of the tree blind and stalked after them to the slack Slimy River. On the muddy banks they disrobed and waded one by one into the river until they disappeared. They were underwater noodlers! They went to the abyss for catfish.

Suddenly an old bald hunk, undoubtedly a shaman of the tribe, emerged from the murky waters of the Slimy holding a five-foot flopping channel catfish at his waist and shouting as if possessed by the gift of tongues. The initiates and elder noodlers rushed toward their screaming leader and fought to remove the phallocentric fish from his groin.

At this moment, one of the Kylers found me and yanked me away. Thus, I do not know with certainty what took place later that night. However, it was undoubtedly chauvinistic and sexist. Not a single woman was there. Even in the depths of the Slimy River, there is a glass floor through which no woman or girl may descend.

Though my research is incomplete, my initial study shows such promise that it will be published next year by Mulhouse University Press.

Jeff Friedman

PowerPoint Presentation

When I slid my finger over the trackpad and clicked, everyone was snoring loudly and snorting. This was the first time I had used PowerPoint to present my work, so I wasn't sure what I had done wrong. On the screen a plump poet with red cheeks was reciting a poem in the spring, while squirrels clung to the branches and a downy woodpecker banged its beak into the knot in a tree. Where was my photo of Robert Frost sitting in the library?

I clicked again. Now everyone in the audience was eating cotton candy, wisps of pink sticking to their cheeks. Where did they get that stuff?

George Jims jabbed a finger at the screen and burst into staccato guffaws that doubled him over. Jilly Cockburn and Sam Sylvan, dean of the business school, rolled on the printer room floor with hungry hands in each other's underwear, moaning and making yum yum noises.

I jumped back as if I had touched a hot stove. How had this video replaced the one of Obama eating a piece of deep-dish pizza and talking about multi-ethnic America?

Jilly rose from her seat. "You'll be hearing from my lawyer, pal. And you can bet the dean will have something to say about this also."

When I clicked the trackpad again, an owl shot across the room, snagging a mouse then perching on the ledge of the partition to eat its prey. The chewing and crunching were amplified through the speakers. I clicked again, because there were so many vegetarians in the room. If only I could get to the video of Paul Krugman, my presentation might still end on a high note, but now came all the animals in twos entering the ark, came the fire from the sky, the terrible rains and the awful smell, came the dove and the rainbow and the feathers falling.

The screen went blank.

As my colleagues sprang to their feet, I closed out of PowerPoint and tried to shut down. On Tuesday I'd have a long talk with Gretchen in IT, who helped me set up my computer, about the glitches in the presentation.

"Not so fast," ordered Carmine Carmello, chair of our department. "Your hour isn't up yet."

Then came the Q&A.

Ravi Shankar

The Furry Falls in Love

Sometime after Scooter Scutaro had his first chinstrap mishap and before he regretted wearing a thong, he concluded that the furry lifestyle has its limitations. He experienced a lucid flash of insight that made him realize something essential about human nature, but just as he was about to reflect upon it, someone flung a cup of Dr. Pepper at him and his epiphany vanished as sugary fizz dribbled through the mesh mouth that served as both his only air source and his sole view to the outside world. What was it about a molded plastic camel that made people want to pelt its humps?

But then, dear God no, the field house filled with *Who let the dogs out (woof, woof, woof, woof!)* and someone was shoving Scooter toward the pulsating lights and unsteady pyramid of cheerleaders. Sleeping wrapped in bearskin during August in the Everglades would have been cool compared to the sauna trapped inside his suit. If he had peed himself, he wouldn't have been able to tell. Scooter gyrated his humps spasmodically, like he was trying to put a fire out with his ass. The crowd went wild, roaring camera flashes and dog whistles.

It had started out so innocently.

Furries are people who like to dress up in animal costumes. Not all furries are plushies, who like cuddly toys, sometimes specially adapted for pleasure, like the unicorn with the miracle horn, or the teddy who can hardly bear it, but most plushophiles are furries. Dirty furverts. Like the ones at a Fur Convention yiffing in a huge collective pile until their fur is matted with spooge and they have transcended their individual selves to lounge in an upper echelon of enlightened post-bodily awareness.

Scooter, only son of Vespa Scutaro, famed condiment collector of Staten Island, happened to be a furry *and* a plushy, but generally didn't go in for anything more than your usual petting, hugging and skritching. Just light scratching and grooming, like you might do with your friends at a social gathering.

So when he answered the ad looking for "an energetic keeper of the spirit stick" who got to wear a hirsute camel suit, he had thought it would be the perfect opportunity to meet some new furry friends.

After days of tingly anticipation for the first game, Scooter jammed his body into the vacuum-formed ABS plastic head of a grinning camel and pranced out in front of a gymnasium full of rabid Division III basketball fans chanting "Airball! Airball" in unison every few possessions.

Scooter was bummed.

Not a single furogenous zone to tickle, no one to give his humps a proper rubdown. What good was wearing oversize leathery kneepads, if he couldn't spend the afternoon kneeling? But no, he was required to dance on command during the timeouts, working up such lather that his whole celery stalk body would grow sodden before he could take a breath.

Then he glimpsed the lovely furry grizzly, the divine visiting mascot. She had oversize bear paws and foam in all the right places. He saw his chance and busted a move, slaloming his way towards her, oversized head swaying, cloven hoofs thumping, damp fingers desperately working the furry paws to push aside the popcorn vendors and little girls squealing to high-five him. *Away, trollops!* He stiff-armed them aside mercilessly, his Bactrian body undulating, his vision blurred with high fructose corn syrup, until he arrived at the she-bear's side, primed for action.

She wiggled; he waggled. She raised the roof; he picked strawberries. She roared; he reared up and went for it, grabbing at her haunches like the Alpha Furry. He had never felt more yiffy, ripe and ready for some hot fur-on-fur friction. He had bonded with frogs and ferrets, Hello Kitties and Smurfettes, but never a grizzly, never in front of so many cheering fans egging him on. In harried lust he thrust and parried, flounced and pounced, feeling the synthetic fibers on his body vibrate with keen purpose. Yes! Oh yes! Oh sweet mother of Minnie Mouse!

Scooter was in thrall, about to unleash the beast, when his legs were swept out from under him and he crashed, humps-first, to the bottom of the bleachers. Two burly security guards pinned him to the hardwood. He looked back at his mascot mate, her paw clawing the air in a sad but lascivious farewell. This, Scooter realized while dragged kicking from the arena, had to be true love.

Claudia Ward-de León

Six Reasons Why That Waitressing Job Didn't Work Out

1.

Because I "forgot" to tell the kitchen the guy at table ten didn't want onions on his chopped salad. I remembered you from the week before, buddy, and since you "forgot" to tip me, I "forgot" you hate onions.

2.

Because I didn't help sing "Happy Birthday" to the group at table three. I can't help it if Josef the dishwasher and I got into an engaging conversation about Bulgarian food at the wrong time. I was brave enough to try the tarator soup he brought in, but the nettle soup... Nettles? Isn't that what you get on your socks when you go hiking? He always tells me we Americans are so picky.

3.

Because I neglected to get bread over to the sappy lovebirds at table six. All that gazing into each other's eyes and footsies under the table told me they probably wouldn't make it through their tuna tartare without sneaking out to the closest alley. Maybe I'd broken up with my boyfriend earlier that week and maybe I was still feeling bitter about it.

4.

Because the hostess and I never let our manager know that Mandy was running late. Not like her running late was anything new. And did she always serve customers the wrong food? You bet she did. Snuck out every night without rolling clean silverware, too, and somehow she always got away with everything. If it hadn't been for the fact that she was sleeping with the executive chef, she wouldn't even have a job. Well, the sleeping with the executive chef is really just a rumor, which, by the way, you didn't hear from me.

5.

Because I snuck out to smoke a dube with Kurt, the house band's piano player. Can anyone blame us? The poor guy had to sing "Copacabana" every night and me, I had to work six days in a row. One of those shifts was to cover Mandy because she "sprained" her ankle. Like Kurt told me when we were crammed into his steamy-windowed Ford Focus, "a little of the blessed herb makes the experience more tolerable."

6.

Because Julio and I didn't brew a fresh pot of coffee for the lingering octogenarians at table 12. To quote Julio: There's a Starbucks next door, people. But more importantly, the restaurant has been closed for over an hour and you're all still here.

Ken McPherson

The Big Catch

I answered the front door anxious to meet my blind date, Gil. He wasn't truly a blind date; we had gotten to know each other through an online dating service.

Yes, initially I felt a mix of embarrassment and desperation, but the dating site had a professional process everyone had to follow. The possibility of risk didn't seem any larger than the possibility of happiness. As my parents never tired of telling me, there are plenty of fish in the sea.

When I opened the door I was a bit startled to discover Gil was a fish, in fact the largest fish I had ever been this close to. Upright he approached 6 feet tall. I was taught to be open-minded and willing to take a chance now and then, but I honestly lost a beat before I could speak.

"Molly? I'm so pleased to finally meet you."

"Me, too, Gil. Although . . . I must admit I'm a little surprised."

"Because I'm a Carp?"

"No, no. Because your online profile said you weigh 200 pounds, but you have to be at least 300. You're huge."

"What can I say? Baitfish have been plentiful."

He remained standing at the doorway, but I didn't feel comfortable inviting him in. After all, I had no idea of the correct etiquette. Besides, he was dripping water.

"You claimed online that weight didn't really matter," Gil reminded me.

"Well, I guess that makes us both loose with the truth."

Gil turned to go. I looked at the sunlight glinting on his scales and the sexy hump on his back.

"Wait! Don't leave yet. Talk to me."

He turned back to the doorway. I couldn't help but be attracted to his uniqueness, but I also thought about the falsehoods in his online profile. He said he was a good swimmer, and that he was in a large school. The question is whether he intentionally led me on.

"Do you hate all fish," he asked tersely, "or just Carp?"

"I'm not prejudiced! I was just surprised by your size."

"My mother always said I was shapely," he said, looking down at his gently waving ventral fins.

"But I can't get my arms around you. Of course . . . I'm not sure I want to put my arms around an oily fish."

"No need to get ugly, Molly. If you don't like my kind, why did you register at BigCatch.com, then agree to go on a date with me?"

"I didn't know that the site was for fish. You sounded compatible. I pushed myself to take a chance. Look, I'm sorry. Maybe online dating was not a rational decision on my part."

I reached up and touched his mouth, wishing he would stop making that fish-out-of-water, air-sucking lips movement.

I should have closed the door, but I hated rejecting anyone almost as much as I hated being rejected.

"No disrespect, but if I were searching for a fish to date, I would probably choose a trout."

"Trout?" His fins spread out like a preacher's arms. "They are so overrated."

"A rainbow trout," I said, not realizing I was making matters worse.

His tail fin slapped the ground. "Sorry," he said immediately. "I didn't mean to do that."

"Is it an involuntary motor function?" I asked. "I have those, too."

"You see," he said, "we have something in common." His round, glassy eyes grew larger. "You know, with a little makeup I think I could look like a rainbow trout."

"I'm sorry, I really am, but I'm just not ready to make an evolutionary leap."

I gripped the doorknob, guilt rumbling inside me. "You should go before my father's curiosity brings him out here. He's watching *The Sunday Angler*, and I can't promise how he'll react to having you in the doorway, let alone dating his daughter."

"May I contact you again through BigCatch.com?" he asked, his eyes emotionless.

I hesitated. "Just a sec." I went inside for my company's business card and handed it to him. He struggled to hold it under a pectoral fin.

"You can call me direct," I said.

"Thank you." He looked at the card. "So you're in the fertilizer business?"

"Is that a problem?"

"I'll call you," he said on his way down the sidewalk.

Mary Ann Back

Stiff Willy

Willy perched on the edge of his barstool, preparing to pounce, eyes darting for prey across the bar. He caught his own reflection bathed in the golden glow of a neon Bud sign and paused to pay tribute. He was the essence of masculinity, the chick whisperer. Here, at the multiplex bars of the Metropolitan Hotel, he was the Alpha. He marked his territory with tractor-beam pheromones, basking in the glory of his Willyness.

Wednesday was ladies night at both the Stardust Room and the Galaxy A-Go-Go. So certain was he of success, he never rented his own room. He simply targeted travelling businesswomen to scratch his itch in the rooms their employers paid for.

Unsuspecting quarry wandered by—an aging blonde, formerly pretty, emitting the sweet, lingering scent of desperation. She'd separated from the herd. A drop of drool plinked his drink coaster. He adjusted his toupee and went for the kill.

"Excuse me, Miss. Did you know your eyes are brighter than the stars above?"

This was his signature line. Willy raised his eyes soulfully to the planetarium-like ceiling of the Stardust.

The blonde attempted a girlish giggle that sounded like a cross between a wheezing Lon Chaney and a Canada goose.

"Hi! My name's Brandy. What's yours?"

Alpha Willy triumphed again, though she wasn't much of a challenge. He had her key to room 321 within half an hour. He nuzzled her neck and excused himself to visit his dying mother at the nursing home before lights out. He'd let himself in with her key when he returned. She swore she'd wait up. Blowing her a kiss, he strolled to the Galaxy A-Go-Go with the hope he could trade up.

• • •

Victoria had downed three Mojitos in less than an hour. The bartender at the Galaxy gave her a great pour; maybe because Victoria was hot or maybe because she looked like she needed it. Either way was fine, since catching her husband with their neighbor's wife right before flying out on business made death by alcohol sound inviting. But first things first. Victoria vowed to lay the next man she saw. She didn't have to look far. The cheesiest, toupee-headed bottom dweller she'd ever seen walked in. She considered waiting for the next guy. But a vow was a vow.

"Hi, I'm Victoria. Buy me a drink and I'll give you the night of your life."

She winked at him, crossed her long slender legs and smiled provocatively, sitting tall so that her breasts strained against the buttons of her blouse.

He leered at her, licking his lips as if she were a ham sandwich.

"My name's Willy. I like a woman who knows what she wants, 'specially when it's Stiff Willy here. What're you drinking, Victoria?"

Willy? Did he say Stiff Willy? She laughed, snorting her drink up her nose. Regaining her composure, she took his face in her hands and shushed him. "Willy, why ruin the moment with words? If you want to do me, just follow me to my room. But no more talking. At all. Ever."

• • •

Phil? Bill? Shit, what was his name? Victoria rolled over and moaned, bloated from alcohol, regret, and after-sex room service. A vague dread gnawed at her gut.

"Hey Willy, wake up," she said.

No answer.

"Dude, you have to leave."

She shook him hard, anxious for him to be gone. He flopped over toward her, eyes void and as glazed as a frozen tuna's.

"Oh, Sweet Jesus!" she screamed, slamming her pillow over his face.

Victoria sprang from the bed and sprawled onto the floor. Rummaging through his pants pockets, she found his room key. She trussed Willy like a turkey onto the lower shelf of the room service cart, then draped the tablecloth on top, rolled him down the hall to room 321, and dragged him into bed. She hurried back to her room, packed, cancelled her meeting and got the hell out of Dodge.

• • •

Brandy sat poolside sipping her coffee, hoping the sun's rays would heal her shattered ego. She'd waited all night for Willy to return. Such a fool. Her last tear shed, she returned to her room and found Willy naked, sprawled face down, resting peacefully in her bed, with a room service cart alongside. He'd ordered them breakfast! She licked her lips. Let him rest for now; she wanted him primed. It had been a long time since she'd had a good Stiff Willy.

Stefon Mears

Just a Stage

The roar of the explosion pulled my attention from the morning comics. I held my breath, mouth still full of cereal and milk.

"Honestly, can't you boys get along?" asked my mother. I held up a forestalling hand. No sound from the back of the house yet. Then I could hear the rubble shifting. My head drooped as I turned back to breakfast.

"What'd you use?" asked my dad.

"Plastique in the doorframe, with a pressure trigger. He's gotten too good at spotting my trip wires."

Dad chuckled and shook his head, but Mom clucked her tongue, muttering something over the eggs she scrambled for Dad. I think she would have said more, but my brother strolled into the kitchen, giving me a smirk as he brushed the last of the dust off his T-shirt.

"Not bad, squirt," he said, "but not good enough." He poured himself a glass of orange juice and snagged a piece of toast off Dad's plate. He smiled at me again, leaning against the counter with his mouth full of whole wheat and butter. He tossed back the rest of the orange juice, set his glass in the sink. "But I've had three whole years of life to learn tricks you've never thought of." I felt my throat start to close. My face warmed while my hands chilled. "Bet you didn't notice that I'd poisoned your box of cereal instead of the milk."

He laughed as I scrambled for my secret cache of antidotes. If I could get to them in time.

"That is enough, you two!" shouted my mother.

"Now, dear," said my father, "my brother and I were the same way at their age."

Tara L. Masih

Cornucopia

Thanksgiving, Dad came home drunk for dessert. He left after Uncle Bob kept braggin' about the new toilet seat he'd put in for Aunt Betty, who kept snap-snapping the celery and sniffing Mom's food. And I could see Mom was in such a bad mood—she had to say grace for the first time in five years 'cause it was her turn—and she sat there thinking of things to thank God for. And she sat there, and she finally thanked Him for the family being all together, after Dad cleared his throat. When Mom said that, Aunt Betty smiled and winked and Little Bob dropped his spoon in the mashed potatoes and they flew all over her purple silk blouse like white snow, and Mom tried not to smile. And then Grammy asked what time it was and Dad said time to eat and Little Joey laughed and shot a pea bullet at Little Bob with his fork, and no one saw so he shot another and it hit the wall and went splat and Mom glared at Aunt Betty who slapped Little Joey's shaved head. And Uncle Bob said how his son'd be a good recruit and Dad said what was so great about that? Here goes, I thought, and I stabbed my peas, trying to get them on my fork all at once. And I stabbed and got three, then squished them around in the gravy. Here goes, just like at Easter when Aunt Betty had said that she was a reborn-again Christian Scientist, and Dad had said, Figures. I looked up at the expression on Mom's face, and told myself to go look at my own face in the bathroom mirror after dinner. And Uncle Bob said Dad was just jealous because he'd gone to work instead of the army, Wasn't that right, Mom? And Grammy made sucking baby noises with the yams and asked what time it was. And Dad poured more wine and Mom made a stopping face and Dad banged the bottle down so that an apple in the centerpiece, a horn of plenty, rolled toward the crystal salt shaker and knocked it over. And Aunt Betty grabbed a pinch between purple nails and threw it over her right shoulder on the carpet, and Mom picked up the shaker and bumped it down. And Little Joey dropped the turkey drumstick on the floor and he crawled under the table and Dad said, Why would I be jealous about training to shoot men? And Uncle Bob said, It was a hell of a lot more than that! And Mom turned to Aunt Betty and asked how her cantaloupe diet was working, and then Uncle Bob was calling Dad a pinko and Dad was calling him a bastard, and Grammy choked on her yams when she heard bastard, and Mom pounded her on the back and glared at Dad, and then Little Joey started sticking his hand up my skirt under the table and Grammy asked, What time is it! after a glass of wine and Dad said, Time for me to leave.

That was the night Dad came home drunk for dessert.

Steve Deutsch

Cousin Myron and the IRS

I'm sure you all recognize my cousin Myron, aspiring author, GED diplomat, trickster and idiot savant—with not so much savant. Myron is a whiz with numbers and anything related to numbers. He called me the other day as I was urging myself to sit down to do my taxes.

"Why don't you let me do them?" he said with much hurt in his voice.

"Because you'll get me audited. You'll get me fined and imprisoned, perhaps even executed."

I was being stubborn and I knew it. Myron does taxes for the whole family. In fact, he does the taxes for most of the neighborhood, in a thriving and growing business. He stands by his work and his clients, much like a faithful Labrador retriever, which I remark whenever I can, he more than resembles. Not one of his clients has so far been fined, imprisoned or executed and his work is so meticulous that they have rarely been audited.

But Myron will be Myron. He's no CPA, doesn't even have an accounting degree, and when it came time to name his company—for the sign in the storefront, wedged comfortably between Botánica La Bonita and Tiny's Tattoos, up on Pitkin Avenue—he chose CLOSE ENOUGH ACCOUNTING. Every time I consider bringing my forms to Myron, I get a picture of the line just below my signature, asking for "firm's name."

"I'm being audited next Tuesday," Myron said, sounding a bit put out. "I want you to go with me."

"Why not?" I said, though I could give lots of reasons. But there's not much I wouldn't do for Myron, even if visiting the IRS for an inquisition ranks right up there with kicking the bucket on my to-do list.

"Do they have the goods on you?" I asked, trying to sound like Tony Soprano.

"Of course not, you moron!" he screamed. "I'm worried that I might lose my temper."

Myron has reason to worry. Many of my relatives, and I'm sure quite a few of yours, have on occasion thrown a waiter or two through a plate glass window, but Myron is the only one I have ever known to throw a waiter through the window both ways. He chucked some poor schmuck, who was late with his fries then tried to defend his tardiness, through the window to the street, then stepped out, picked him up and heaved him inside again.

When Myron bought me breakfast that morning, I took the waitress aside and warned her. She survived. We got to the IRS at about 9 and took a number. It wasn't until after 11 that an auditor was free to speak to us. Myron and the auditor sparred for two and a half hours. After that, Myron worked over the supervisor for another ninety minutes. When asked a question, Cousin Myron would quote something like, "Section 78, Paragraph 2, Line 101." Gradually, through the stupor that had become my life in the IRS office, I began to realize that Myron had memorized the tax code, and could quote it like a preacher does the Old Testament.

When we finally left, I couldn't help offering Myron a bit of enlightenment.

"If you don't want to be audited every year, change the name of your business to something less IRS offensive."

Myron gave me one of those long, sad looks people usually reserve for Mets fans.

"What are you talking about? I love getting audited. I look forward to it every year."

"Please don't tell me you have the whole tax code memorized."

Myron saluted. "Guilty as charged."

"How long is it?" For some reason I actually wanted to know.

"16,845 printed pages," he said. "Want to hear it?"

"For the love of God, no." At that moment my mind felt queasier but easier as I realized that aside from Myron, the best anyone can ever do in filing taxes is to be close enough.

"OK," I said, "how'd you like to do my taxes?"

Myron grinned like a man who would never throw a waiter through a window.

"Fine, but it will cost you big bucks. We are talking about three lunches at Katz's Deli—lean corned beef on rye, two potato knishes, and a Dr. Brown's cream soda. Plus dessert if I get you a refund."

"Deal," I said, thinking as we shook hands that he'd probably opt for the cheesecake.

Sherrie Flick

Learning to Drink Coffee in Idaho

I called to request a coffeemaker and some of those E-Z packets you just plop right in, no mess.

"Mr. Smith? We don't do that kind of shit here," purred the woman's voice from the front desk.

I replaced the receiver and re-dialed, thinking surely I had made a mistake in hitting "0." The same voice again, slight nasal twang to her speech.

"What now?" she asked, still an edge of amusement there at the outer boundaries of her vocal cords.

"Coffee," I said. "Give it to me."

A tiny gasp puffed through the phone's speaker. I have to admit to feeling a surge of feeling all good and manly there for a second.

"Not sure where you're from, sir, but here in Idaho customers don't talk like that to fine-looking, underpaid motel reception desk clerks. Here's what I suggest. You get off your duff and get your own damn coffee."

I nestled the sweaty plastic receiver against my shoulder, looked myself up and down in the full-length motel room mirror. In underwear and socks I didn't look that hot, a little green even. But still, if I sucked in my gut and ditched the socks, someone might look twice. I turned sideways, wondered aloud about speaking with the manager.

"Down the street and to the right. Darlene's Diner. Take yourself for a walk."

She hung up.

Cool, oily air circled the streets as cars and trucks revved into the morning's rush. I followed the clerk's directions, walking immaculate sidewalks that looped together like a long string of Band-Aids. They led straightaway and to the right to a brick wall. I retraced my steps and when looking to the left saw Darlene's. A warm pink neon light perched in the window, whispering *open* in all lowercase. I thought about eggs and coffee and a full refund on my room. I thought about sales and the conference Reg my boss was forcing me to attend in two hours because mine were down.

"Down in the dumps," Reggie had said. "Go do some learning."

Inside the door, Darlene's pink counter stretched out before me, nearly empty except for a few balding heads bobbing behind rumpled newspapers. Darlene herself stood behind the register, scowling. Hands on her hips she drawled out, "Over from the motel, are you?" She sniffed. "Heard about you and what you said to our Peggy."

"Out of context," I said. "How about a truce—or at least some coffee?" I held out my arms to appear beseeching.

My small speech fell like a dead bird in the middle of a line cook's grill. I nodded, trying to remember why this was happening to me. I sat down in a booth, safer it seemed than the exposure of a stool. I nestled in, actually, listened to the country and western playing softly in the kitchen. I waited. It took a long time, but eventually a waitress sauntered my way.

"What have you?" she asked. Her nametag read Betty. "Hurry it up. I've got real customers over there."

"That's a nice dress you have on," I said. "I just want some coffee and a couple eggs. That's all. No trouble."

"Okay," she said. "Your sales are down. Way down, aren't they? What I'm hearing is you want a pecan roll. That's what you need." She scribbled fiercely in her receipt book and strode away, leaving a faint smell of vanilla in her wake.

How Betty knew of my sales tanking was beyond me. Probably that notorious Peggy was listening in when Reg called last night to berate me some more. Betty was right, though. I did need a pecan roll. When the coffee came it rose to the thick cup's rim—dark and beautiful. The pecan roll, served without eggs, tasted earthy and luscious. It reminded me of Alabama—of times before when I'd let loose of myself too much, back when I knew how to beg for more, back when I asked for coffee and got it right away.

I was anxious about asking for a second roll. I checked my watch. I only had so much time before I'd be late for the first session. When Betty refilled my cup, I grabbed my chance. "Possible to have two more eggs?" I asked.

She smiled then, a knowing kind of grin that tipped up at each side a little bit feline. "Now you're getting it," Betty said, tapping the table once for emphasis. "I'll see what I can do."

The second pecan roll came like a miracle perched on a pretty blue plate. I sipped my still-hot coffee. I ate every gooey pecan, pressing my finger on each stray nut and popping it into my mouth. Later, I apologized. I apologized to everyone, every single person in the diner. I shook Darlene's hand on my way out. I got down on my knees and proposed marriage to Betty right there and then. She blushed a little, said yes, and then asked if she'd see me tomorrow. "Remember," she said, pulling me up to my feet again. "Sales is all about negotiation. See what they're giving you when they talk and take it, use it against them. It's what we all do. Every day." She kissed me on the cheek and I remembered a few more things from my past.

"Okay. Good," Peggy said when I got back to the motel, handed her the to-go cup that Darlene had pushed into my hand. "Good. I'm thinking you can stay another night."

RANDALL D. BROWN

COMFORTABLE

Before I taught my son old vaudeville jokes, I was a terrible father. For example, one day my son and mother-in-law were looking up planets in her yellowing, moldy World Books. As my son ran in for another volume, I whispered in his ear—and he ran back into the living room.

I leaned back into the couch of the family room, turned off the volume to the Eagles game.

"Grandma," he yelled out, "I want to look up Ur-Anus."

She isn't a stomper, my mother-in-law. Her slippered feet made no sound, really, and she didn't raise her voice.

"Do you want him to get in trouble in school? Do you want him to think he can just blurt out anything anywhere? Do you want to teach him to say anything anyone whispers in his ear?" And so on.

"No," I said. "Of course not. I'm sorry. Wasn't thinking."

And this is just one of a hundred such moments, she reminded me. Wasn't I responsible for his bending over in the bath and saying, "Look Grandma, it's morning. Can you see the crack of dawn?" Or his saying his penis is in trouble, it's got these two nuts following him around. Yes, yes, I say, it's all true. The whole litany of charges.

She shakes her head, blows out a sigh. Incorrigible, sick, a terrible influence on her grandson.

So the next Thanksgiving, my son and I are stuffed, sitting on the couch, watching the game, our hands folded on our bellies, our pants unsnapped.

"Well, well," my mother-in-law says, "you look comfortable."

"I make a living," my son says.

You've never seen such delight in a mother-in-law before. She brings us pie—even warms it up first. A scoop of vanilla ice cream, melting on the top. Lets us eat it on the couch. Says nothing about our stinky feet on her pillows. She smiles, arms folded, as we eat. Takes the plates away.

"I make a living," she repeats. Then picks up the phone. "You'll never guess what my grandson just said."

I wink at my son. He gives me a high-five. We are living large.

"Hey, Grandma," he says, when she hangs up. "I know why Jewish men like Grandpa die before their wives do."

Ah, no. Not that one. Not now.

"They want to."

Ryan Ridge

Shaky Hands & All

I was an unemployed astrologer suffering from writer's block. The stars were bad and I refused to play middleman. Like so many of my fellow horoscope writers, I found myself chasing the narrative arcs of daytime soaps with warm beer and cigarettes, intermittently ambling to the mailbox to fetch my unemployment stipend.

• • •

She was an out-of-work manicurist who'd been wrongfully accused of failing to wash her hands before returning from the bathroom. She quit after union threats. She began reading palms. Career-wise it was profitable, given the state of things.

• • •

We met in the lobby of the Psychic Job Fair, where she summoned me to a little booth near the back of the auditorium. "Your palm reads like a cheap romance novel," she said. She dropped my hand and asked what I was doing later.

• • •

At her place, we drank Robitussin and played strip poker with a deck of Tarot cards. In our skivvies, she gazed directly through my forehead and said: "I see you inside me."

One . . . two . . . three minutes later, I apologized. "Didn't see that coming, did you?"

"No, but I see you buying me breakfast."

"Shake on it," I said.

We reached out to shake hands, but they were already shaking.

Susan Terris

Rhino in the Bedroom

He was small at first and tolerable, like a Steiff toy dragged by one ear and dropped there by one of the children, though he seemed to move from place to place, as her Storybook Dolls had when she was a girl. But soon he began to grow. Her husband, oblivious, walked through the creature, sat on him, covered him with newspapers.

At night, she was aware of the lightning bolt in the rhino's eyes, and she began to feel the tip of his horn at the small of her back, his breath against her face, the indentation of his body on her side of the bed. In short: he was disturbing; but every time she tried to talk with him, he gazed at her, inhaled, and grew larger.

Whenever she mentioned the rhino, her husband said he was late for a meeting, a game, or couldn't hear her over the bounce of the ball on TV. Then the rhino began to brush against her, make noises with his lips, root through her drawers and closets, rub her back, examine her journals. And he continued to grow, until one morning when her husband was at work, the rhino knelt down and, for the first time, spoke.

I love you, he said. *Unconditionally.* No one had ever loved her unconditionally—not parents, husband, or even the children. *I'm subtle, he continued in a husky tone, and conveniently insubstantial. O Beloved, take me into the savannah of your heart.*

Moral: *A person who says size doesn't matter has never had a horny rhinoceros in the bedroom.*

Credits

Kim Addonizio: "But" © 2013 by Kim Addonizio. First appeared in *The Box Called Pleasure, FC2*. Reprinted by permission of the author.

Steve Almond: "Unfriendly Cashiers" © 2013 by Steve Almond. Published by arrangement with the author.

Mary Ann Back: "Stiff Willy" © 2013 by Mary Ann Back. Published by arrangement with the author.

Julianna Baggott: "The Prude Responds to Rock and Roll" © 2013 by Julianna Baggott. Published by arrangement with the author.

Paul Blaney: "Later at Cana" © 2013 by Paul Blaney. Published by arrangement with the author.

Tori Bond: "Swimming with the Chickens" © 2013 by Tori Bond. Published by arrangement with the author.

Randall D. Brown: "Comfortable" © 2013 by Randall Brown. First appeared in *FRIGG*. Reprinted by permission of the author.

Mark Budman: "On Demand" © 2013 by Mark Budman. First appeared in *Raleigh Review*. Reprinted by permission of the author.

Ron Carlson: "Syllabus" © 2013 by Ron Carlson. First appeared in *Washington Square Review*. Reprinted by permission of the author.

Jess Charest: "Mouse" © 2013 by Jess Charest. Published by arrangement with the author.

Matthew Charles: "This City" © 2013 by Matthew Charles. Published by arrangement with the author.

Peter Cherches: "Double Date" © 2013 by Peter Cherches. First appeared in somewhat different form in *North American Review*. Reprinted by permission of the author.

Kelly Cherry: "The Department of Mirth and Laughter" © 2013 by Kelly Cherry. Published by arrangement with the author.

Joe Clifford: "Fair Shake" © 2013 by Joe Clifford. Published by arrangement with the author.

T.J. Coane: "America's Got Smarts!" © 2013 by T.J. Coane. Published by arrangement with the author.

Joey Comeau: "Cover Letter" © 2013 by Joey Comeau. First appeared in *Overqualified*. Reprinted by permission of the author.

Rand Richards Cooper: "El Turista" © 2013 by Rand Richards Cooper. First appeared in *Black Book*. Reprinted by permission of the author.

Ronald G. Crowe: "Brothers and Sisters" © 2013 by Ronald G. Crowe. Published by arrangement with the author.

Jon Davis: "Music Men" © 2013 by Jon Davis. First appeared (as

"Compare and Contrast: Chris Isaak and Van Morrison") in *McSweeney's Internet Tendency.* Reprinted by permission of the author.

Terry DeHart: "Negotiations" © 2013 by Terry DeHart. Published by arrangement with the author.

Steve Deutsch: "Cousin Myron and the IRS" © 2013 by Steven Deutsch. Published by arrangement with the author.

Stuart Dybek: "Fantasy" © 2013 by Stuart Dybek. First appeared in *Joe.* Reprinted by permission of the author.

Roberto G. Fernández: "Wrong Channel" © 2013 by Roberto G. Fernández. First appeared in *Micro Fiction.* Reprinted by permission of the author.

Zac Finkenstein: "The Young Man and the D" © 2013 by Zac Finkenstein. Published by arrangement with the author.

Kathy Fish: "Delivery" © 2013 by Kathy Fish. First appeared in *Boundoff.com.* Reprinted by permission of the author.

Craig Fishbane: "Poets at the Boarding House" © 2013 by Craig Fishbane. First appeared in *Referential.* Reprinted by permission of the editor, Jessie Carty.

Sherrie Flick: "Learning to Drink Coffee in Idaho" © 2013 by Sherrie Flick. Published by arrangement with the author.

Jeff Friedman: "PowerPoint Presentation" © 2013 by Jeff Friedman. First appeared in different form in *Storyscape Literary Journal.* Reprinted by permission of the author.

Steven Gray: "Hansel and Gretel in California" © 2013 by Steven Gray. First appeared in different form in *Shadow on the Rocks.* Reprinted by permission of the author.

John Haggerty: "Outside the Box" © 2013 by John Haggerty. First appeared in *Opium.* Reprinted by permission of the author.

Tom Hazuka: "Sunflowers of Evil" © 2013 by Tom Hazuka. First appeared in longer form in *Drunken Boat.* Reprinted by permission of the author.

Tania Hershman: "The Google 250" © 2013 by Tania Hershman. First appeared in *My Mother Was An Upright Piano: Fictions* (Tangent Books, 2012). Reprinted by permission of the author and Tangent Books.

Arthur Hoppe: "The Waiting Game" © 2013 by Nick Hoppe. First appeared in *The San Francisco Chronicle.* Reprinted by permission of Nick Hoppe.

Nick Hoppe: "How to Waste Two Hours of Life" © 2013 by Nick Hoppe. Published by arrangement with the author.

Adam Johnson: "Denti-Vision Satellite" © 2013 by Adam Johnson. First appeared in slightly different form in *Ninth Letter.* Reprinted by permission of the author.

Robert P. Kaye: "Poison Hotline" © 2013 by Robert P. Kaye. First appeared in *The Journal of Truth and Consequence.* Reprinted by permission of the author.

Scott Lambridis: "The Pile" © 2013 by Scott Lambridis. Published by arrangement with the author.

Ring Lardner: "The Young Immigrunts" original © 1920 by Curtis Publishing Corporation. Currently out of copyright.

Barry H. Leeds: "Not the Bend Over Part" © 2013 by Barry H. Leeds. Published by arrangement with the author.

Frances Lefkowitz: "Dessert for Superman" © 2013 by Frances Lefkowitz. Published by arrangement with the author.

Sean Lovelace: "I Love Bocce" © 2013 by Sean Lovelace. First appeared in *How Some People Like Their Eggs.* Reprinted by permission of Rose Metal Press.

Taylor Mali: "The the Impotence of Proofreading" © 2013 by Taylor Mali. First appeared in *What Learning Leaves.* Reprinted by permission of the author.

Mandy Manning: "Just Outside the Closet" © 2013 by Mandy Manning. First appeared in *Shattering the Glass Slipper.* Reprinted by permission of shatteringtheglassslipper.blogspot.com.

Tara L. Masih: "Cornucopia" © 2013 by Tara L. Masih. First appeared in *Word of Mouth: 150 Short-Short Stories by 90 Women Writers* (Crossing Press, 1990). Reprinted by permission of the author.

Colin McEnroe: "Primitive Man Tames the Wolf" © 2013 by Colin McEnroe. First appeared in *The Hartford Courant.* Reprinted by permission of the author.

Ken McPherson: "The Big Catch" © 2013 by Ken McPherson. Published by arrangement with the author.

Stefon Mears: "Just a Stage" © 2013 by Stefon Mears. Published by arrangement with the author.

Joe Mills: "Toy Story" © 2013 by Joe Mills. First appeared in *Literary Orphans.* Reprinted by permission of the author.

Dinty W. Moore: "Revolution" © 2013 by Dinty W. Moore. First appeared in significantly different form in *Quick Fiction 10* (Spring 2006). Reprinted by permission of the author.

Kona Morris: "I'm Pretty Sure Nicolas Cage Is My Gynecologist" © 2013 by Kona Morris. First appeared in *Fast Forward Press's Flash 101: Surviving the Fiction Apocalypse.* Reprinted by permission of Fast Forward Press and the author.

DovBer Naiditch: "Interview with an Orthodox Jewish Vampire" © 2013 by DovBer Naiditch. Published by arrangement with the author.

Marisela Navarro: "The Defenestration of Prince Eric" © 2013 by Marisela Navarro. Published by arrangement with the author.

Kirk Nesset: "Believing in People" © 2013 by Kirk Nesset. First appeared in *Western Humanities Review*. Reprinted by permission of the author.

Steven Ostrowski: "Willard" © 2013 by Steven Ostrowski. Published by arrangement with the author.

Pamela Painter: "Artist as Guest in the Hamptons" © 2013 by Pamela Painter. First appeared in *Wouldn't You Like to Know*. Reprinted by permission of the author.

David Partenheimer: "Nude Noodling in Slovinger, Missouri" © 2013 by David Partenheimer. Published by arrangement with the author.

Meg Pokrass: "Divorced Devouts' Potluck" © 2013 by Meg Pokrass. First appeared in *failbetter* (Spring 2013). Reprinted by permission of the author.

Shelby Raebeck: "My Hypoglycemic Son and ADD Wife" © 2013 by Shelby Raebeck. Published by arrangement with the author.

Charles Rafferty: "My Yoga Pants, My Executioner" © 2013 by Charles Rafferty. Published by arrangement with the author.

Leslie Rapparlie: "Interview" © 2013 by Leslie Rapparlie. Published by arrangement with the author.

Ryan Ridge: "Shaky Hands & All" © 2013 by Ryan Ridge. First appeared in *Fractured West*. Reprinted by permission of the author.

Bruce Holland Rogers: "Egypt" © 2013 by Bruce Holland Rogers. First appeared in *Funny Times*. Reprinted by permission of the author.

Chuck Rosenthal: "Intimations of Immortality" © 2013 by Chuck Rosenthal. First appeared (as "Roscoe Gets a Phone Call") in *Santa Monica Review*. A version also appeared in *West of Eden* (What Books Press, 2012). Reprinted by permission of the author.

Sarah Russell: "Mother's Last Wishes" © 2013 by Sarah Russell. First appeared in *The Incredible Shrinking Story* (Flash Forward Press). Reprinted by permission of Flash Forward Press and the author.

Robert Scotellaro: "Bookends" © 2013 by Robert Scotellaro. First appeared in *Measuring the Distance* (Blue Light Press/1st World Publishing, 2012). Reprinted by permission of the author.

Ravi Shankar: "The Furry Falls in Love" © 2013 by Ravi Shankar. Published by arrangement with the author.

Gail Louise Siegel: "Author Interview" © 2013 by Gail Louise Siegel. Published by arrangement with the author.

Louise Farmer Smith: "Vita 1985" © 2013 by Louise Farmer Smith. First appeared in *Southeast Review* (Fall 2005). Reprinted by permission of the author.

Printed in the United States of America

Lightning Source UK Ltd.
Milton Keynes UK
UKOW02f1838020816

279812UK00004B/332/P